Psychoboys

Psychoboys
by Bertie Marshall

Psychoboys

Published in May 1997 by

Codex
PO Box 148
Hove
East Sussex
BN3 2UZ
UK

ISBN 1 899598 05 7

Front cover photo: Georgina Ravencroft

Cover boy: Julian Kalinowsky

Author photo: Peter Brown

Acknowledgments and thanks to the following:
Simon Strong, Pete Pavement, Ira Silverberg, Peter Brown,
P. P. Hartnett, Susan J. Curtis, Julian
and to all my friends over the years for their support

Appreciation to Patti Smith and Nico for their inspirational soundtracks.

PSYCHOBOYS is for Stephen Hawthorne with love.

The writing of this book was funded by a grant from SOUTH EAST ARTS

Printed in London, England by The Book Factory

Part I

"Thawing"

As everything is seen in a dream,

thus should one see all things

Chapter I

O N A PSYBERIAN WORK SITE, PSYCHOBOYS ARE ASSEMBLING TOYS, their bellies poking through vests made of hemp – bodies entwined by the narcotic vine. Pale, hairless flesh taut over still growing bones. Not one of them is over sixteen. The boys' meaty hands fumble over intricate parts of toy cars – deconstructed Psycho mechanics.

They are in search of broken things. Most of their families have been murdered, tortured, or have abandoned them through poverty. So the Psychoboys fend for themselves. A gaggle of them packed in ice on a ship: the dead ones stored in salt. The Psychoboys are preserved in ice for a future that is totally uncertain.

In summer, the ice doesn't melt, impacted by a dark rationality. These boys are more impervious than emperor scorpions, more cunning than rats. Their punishment – for what crime exactly? Psychic injuries are received and the boys wear cerebral band aids covering malicious psychic wounds dating back to 1914, 1931, 1966, 1971, 1994.

The council estate, where they lived for a short while, was built on a vast cemetery that was built on a concentration camp. Home was made from other peoples bones. Playing ball with skulls. I don't know where they came from or where they're going: into a No Future. Maybe the PUNK maxim, NO Future was right. Or, perhaps, a future made out of chance.

I just want to clarify that when I say Psychoboys I mean Psychoboy, for I have chosen only one – REZ.

Here is a statement – a tract – on what a Psychoboy is... officially compiled by government officials, men under orders with dark blue shadows for faces and eyes hidden beneath peaked caps. The notice is typed on yellowing paper, littered by the occasional green fly splattered as a full stop.

"A hooligan is a homeless boy, a vagabond, who because of the power of hunger, has become a Psychoboy, a thief, vermin, grimy little criminal – green fly! Without families these sons become homeless... Psychoboys are particularly dangerous if allowed to enter the dream state for long periods of time... it is imperative to keep these hooligans from dreaming."

The Psychoboys are in the bowels of the ship now. One movement of lean muscled aggression, brutal, violet-eyed, all their senses sharpened by years of deprivation. Kids who would do well living on Pluto, the furthest planet from the sun.

In the dark recess of the ship's hold, Rez is dreaming with his eyes open. He is looking out from his block of ice. The cold gnaws at his bones. His eyes move with the flitting jerk of an insect's eye. A billowing white sail wavers over the horizon, like a sheet from a hospital. Rez begins a tiny, almost imperceptible, thaw. And as he does a film plays across his eyes. Two cowboys walk into a saloon twirling guns, they aim at each other, come face to face, drop their jeans and point the muzzles up one another's arses and blow each other away.

Rez twitches at the vision, it is out of his sphere of reference. The words to a song play in his brain... here's a translation in English... what he hears...

"Red ice, tearing at him like thunder,

ripping it open and all asunder,

sixteen dancing sailors fell,

a rope, a lover's denial, well...

some one waved a wand, and then they were gone."

Rez's astral body inflates to gigantic size, he rises, leaving the bowels of the ship, floating above Okhotsk Ocean. From Rez's lofty point of view, the ship looks like a piece of crumpled up paper, dipping and swirling about in a puddle.

Inside his huge self, amid the snowy wastes, an internal monologue is thawing in his native tongue. My function is to translate from his silence via my pen. Now he is flying sleepily. I watch his thoughts descend ever downward, dropping like ice cubes... clink... clink... clink... in the grey briny.

REZ: "My past so twisted and I'm not sixteen yet… standing on street corners sipping watery Vodka from my flask, waiting for any dirty old fucker to offer me 30 roubles for a blow job… peppered vodka to chase away the salty taste of cum… the ship from up here looks like a speck of dust in a tear. My heart feels like it's splintering.

I remember standing in the doorway of a bakery. One night this Sailor walks up to me and offers me 20 roubles for a blow job… there was something unreal about him and beautiful, and I'm not into guys that way, I'm not into anybody that way, I just do it for money or drugs… something in his eyes, it was like he reflected part of me.

The sailor gave me the 20 roubles and said: "I've been away a long time". I remember those words, because they were the only ones he spoke. Before I had time to go down on him, he pushed me deep into the doorway, hard kisses, breathing garlic and vodka fumes, his sweaty face sliding up and down mine… he fell against me, full force, his weight pulverising me like a steel girder, it felt like god was tonguing me… he drove his hands under my sweater full of holes, pinching my nipples till they hurt… I couldn't breathe, his cock made an arc in his pants, nodding, bowing, rush of sighs, and like an atomic blast he came and vanished before my eyes… "I've been away a long time".

Rez falls into a silence that I cannot translate. It is opaque, plummets down and down, fathoms, five, where maybe now his father lies.

Action man

Standing to attention behind the cellophane window of a cardboard box, in a white cotton sailor suit, painted black crop, lightly tanned, eyes of improbable blue – blank gaze and thin lips (Mother said never trust them). Action man is waiting for me to unwrap him.

I strip all half-metre of him, he doesn't resist, a brass band plays "76 Trombones" on the radio. I'm amazed at his body, neat, shiny muscles, cartoon torso and biceps, all that worked out hard plastic. But no cock! Only a smooth pinky-brown lump that looks like a cough sweet. I pull his legs apart. NO BALLS! I stare down at the discarded uniform, little heaps of white cotton, too small to try on so I pocket them for misuse later. Like the good sailor he is, he stares straight ahead, not flinching.

I give him a two second caress, the time it takes my index finger to slide the length of his body. Nothing stirs. I put him down on the bed and lay next to him. I pull his arms about so they are folded under his head, he looks great, small but great. I roll on my side and kiss his lips, but instead engulf his entire face... he doesn't move, which starts to annoy me. I put my head on his chest and he sinks about three inches into the bed. He feels cool, hard and finally insubstantial.

He lays there gazing at the ceiling.

Rez still floating in silence: I manage to capture one oblique sentence as it spills "These eerie words words words on a long long road where at last my boots are worn in." Strange beautiful thoughts.

Action man lying prostrate. I touch him again, he is too cold to be my lover now. I push him off the bed, he lands on his stomach with a plastic thud... clack... his neck twisted like it's broken. Yes, it's a terrible thing to be rejected, you may say he's only a toy / doll / boy / man, but I really can't forgive him… his silence.

The petrol spews out of the lighter refill can in a shower covering and sliding off his back and down to the crack of his bum… I squeeze the last drops out of the can and crumple it, it makes a hiss crack sound, I hurl it into the waste paper bin. I pick up my doused Action man and plop him into the bin, fumbling about for a light – taking a match from a box with a drawing of a Boxer dog on it. Maybe what I need is a dog, devoted, attentive, obedient.

Action man is slumped against the side of the bin, his legs akimbo, head crooked – same old expression.

The match flares up in my fingers as I shriek my hex "Happy burning, baby!" The match plummets, igniting him, flames jump right away and smother him. The eyes are the first to go, peeling away to black tar, head shrivels, all his musculature melting into sticky bubbles, left foot withered to a speck of shit grey blobbiness. The smell is unbelievable.

I look down at the atrocity and at my hands, fingers, I notice that the 'moons' on my nails above the cuticle are only half-visible crescents; partial eclipses. A sure sign of schizophrenia.

S OMETHING INSIDE OF REZ SNAPS, HIS ASTRAL BODY SLOWLY deflates, a pinprick to his ballooning self.

Memories of his mother come flooding back – he sees the last apartment where they lived. His father, absent without leave? Rez returns to the apartment like a haunting.

Rez's mother fashioned herself on the Greek legend – Medea. She was a drama queen of the first order. She was known to wander along the corridor of the apartment singing like a strangled peacock, snatches of arias, inaudible, blurring languages, bending notes – like I said – a peacock being strangled.

The corridor was littered with withered arms that she had collected from the death-pits that pockmarked the boundaries of the council estate where they lived. For some insane reason she called them her *army of arms*. She couldn't decide whether they were trophies or would come in handy for something one day.

You could see the extent of her insanity by the clothes she draped herself in: usually a natty pink towelling robe, with her hair a shag-pile of grey locks on which perched, precariously, a rhinestone tiara (it actually looked like or was an old bird-cage decorated with bits of silver thread). She often screamed at Rez: "Call me princess". She thought she was a descendent of Nick and Alex. Beneath Medea's natty robe she wore a holster and two guns, she'd got them off the black market, in fact she had traded Rez's dad for them. He was one bang she was glad to get rid of. The two pearl handled guns she called "gunettes", for she was camp as only people who emulate queens are. She invented a game to kill time, for she seriously thought it would be better to attempt to kill time than let time kill her. The game she invented was RUSSIAN ROULETTE.

Periodically she would chase Rez up and down the corridor and around the apartment, brandishing the gunettes, her light blue eyes rolling wildly in her head, she spat and twirled the guns at Rez... click... twirl... click... screeching peacock... she aimed and fired at a mirror already cracked.

Once upon a time, she fired a bullet through the wooden floor where it shattered an old lady's set of false teeth as they lay chattering on a bedside table.

Suddenly a gigantic pair of scissors appeared and cut up the memory of his mother, scattering her far and wide like confetti, or frames of a lost film.

Chapter 2

REZ MET THE LOVE OF HIS TWISTED LIFE IN A MOSCOW NIGHTCLUB called The Elysian Fields also known as 'The Toilet'. The club looked like an empty aeroplane hanger – concrete coffin with a false sky, bewildering grid of astral spotlights. The floor was a trough of sleaze, spilt beer, cigarette stubs, broken poppers bottles. In the centre of the dancefloor a human gyroscope flashed in firework colours of fluorescent green and pink, turning its passenger upside down and inside out. The young man strapped inside made a thousand or so bizarre grimaces, turning him every which way but loose, spinning him into queer stratospheres.

Rez stands alone with only 2 roubles in his pocket. The midnight ritual – incense burning, taped music of monks chanting – sweeps across the dancefloor. Rez is looking at his 'lover to be' who has stopped spinning and clambers out of the gyroscope, totally spaced, a statue of perplexity. Rez's 'lover' is really a mirror image, blond crop, violet-eyed, but taller than Rez – softer face. In this twilight world the lover stares, piercing Rez's heart and temples. The crown, at the top of his head, is sending lightning bolts down into his solar plexus and along the purple vein on his cock. They are fixated by each other – energy runs between them in matrix currents: circuits.

Rez walked forward and so did the lover, under a galaxy of spotlights they merged. The Psychoboys collided their identities in some sort of consensual hallucination.

The toilets of The Elysian Fields were really nothing more than a quagmire of piss, shit and semen.

Rez and the lover tiptoe through the concrete cauldron, passing queers that are laying face down in the bog. The smell is abysmal. They are seeking some quiet corner to commune. In the squelching squalor, beneath arcs of sputum they wade to a darker corner. And not a word is spoken. Their first touches send torrents of endorphines cascading through their nervous systems, buffeting the shock of rage which is indistinguishable from the passion they feel. As they kiss for the first time their instincts make them want to punch one another, in brutal affection, or in competition of who will be 'boss'. The soles of their boots are taking in the effluence from the floor, so very soon they're glued to the ground.

Rez's and the lover's tongues invade – curling and lapping inside each other's mouths. They play 'Swallow the Oyster' which consists of hacking up globs of phlegm and spitting them down each others' throats.

Rez can smell the scent of *Genet,* an Eau de Colonge, on the lover's neck – a charming little sniff of squashed crab lice, vaseline, blood, sperm and shredded wool spun from the uniforms of prisoners. Sold in little pink glass bottles shaped like a cock-and-balls – a dab behind each ear or bollock and one is assured of picking up rough trade.

Suddenly Rez and the lover pull away, as two burly Cossacks enter the scene, in their fine furry hats and shiny black boots like two grizzly bears in winter drag, they stomp the length of the cavern of piss and shit, marching in unison, cartoonesque, handlebar moustaches twitching – holes for eyes – like someone has put their lights out and their batteries are slowly wearing down. They are useless shells without command, survivors of an army long gone. Ancestors of ice.

The *Genet* fumes are intoxicating, Rez feels something, what is it his young soul is seeking? The lover and he are face to face casting meticulous shadows over one another, their pale flesh flushing pink, nipples swirl like cosmic eyes beneath their clothes of holes, flashes of skin peeping through, tongues dive again and Rez is lost.

In one of the cubicles someone pulls a chain and Rez's thoughts return to the ship riding the waves on the Okhotsk ocean. Lights twinkling in his eyes as thoughts of death wing their way in from grey clouds. A jangling memory... his mother being taken away by the Police for hanging herself upside down on a hook in a butcher's shop.

Rez comes back to the present and the lover who is fading into the shadows. Rez watches him dematerialise to a fuzzy black aura.

Rez thinks: "We only exist as long as we hang together."

Rez, caught in this disintegrating hallucination, in this device called memory... stealing a postcard from the bookshop next to the butcher's shop where his mother was hanging... a postcard from England, a childlike drawing of two boys that look like bags or stones in a network of wire... on the back, the inscription in English: "WE TWO BOYS TOGETHER CLINGING".

The lover is gone, almost. Out of the corner of Rez's violet eyes he becomes a beautiful wavy line. Rez knows there is nothing he can do except experience this moment without loss, without any kind of pain. It will be simply filed away at the back of his brain as a 'Brainiac Amour'... a mind fuck.

Chapter 3

REZ HAD NEVER KNOWN SCHOOL BOOKS, HE COULD BARELY READ OR write, but he was adept at dreaming. He had learned everything from being on the streets, stealing and selling sex. He had all the sharp sleazy instincts of a guttersnipe. He had no heroes or heroines. Women appeared to him as different faces, facets, hideous distorting mirrors of his poor mad mother. With no idols or icons to worship, Rez remained uninspired and aspired to nothing, to no-one. Survival was the name of his game. Memories linked him to a dismal past... there is a kind of freedom in being lost, without roots. Going nowhere can mean you are going anywhere.

The Elysian Fields was in fact nothing more than a mirage. A railway arch littered with human debris, a slag heap of body parts into which he had hallucinated himself – a virtual landscape. He looked at the floor. In the gutter a navy blue rope lay curled in a figure of eight – infinity.

Rez fading in and out of situations. Passing through levels of paper and ink. This means Rez is in perpetual escape from his childhood... like me at that age he felt older than his years, yet he was still stuck on the corner of his childhood. Rez was half angel, half genie... a genie without a bottle.

The drugs he liked to take when he could afford them, or most often steal them, were ones that anaesthetised him. He picked up this taste at birth, when his mad mother had given the anaesthetist a blow job on the delivery table in exchange for a sniff of the anaesthetic. The sleeping gas was not available to the poor or demented. Rez had to be cut out Caesarean style – ripped and gassed, born asleep, stoned. The nurse had to spank him into existence. He was born with his beautiful violet eyes open, but open to a permanent blur. His world was one of somnolent platitudes, of holograms that orbit about his gorgeous blond head, cosmic garlands, waiting: waiting to be decoded... telling His Story.

Chapter 4

THE JUDGE THAT SENTENCED REZ TO ICE WAS A FAT TOAD, DEWLAP upon dewlap ran down his face, he wore a fur hat beneath which little grey ringlets poked out, a black satin eye patch concealed his left eye. (There was nothing wrong with his left eye, he just preferred it be 'eclipsed' – an appendage of mystery!) From his right eye emanated a very fruity glint.

The Judge sat in the court room, a rose exquisitely clenched between his teeth, swung round on his chair like a kid on a swing… he was known in the profession as *Miss Igor*.

He had a hard task sentencing Rez as he was a former client. He loved nothing more than to be put in a cage and 'Lion-tamed' which, put simply, meant Rez would go to his house and lock the Judge – Miss Igor – in a kid's playpen (the cage) and flay him with a washing line (the whip) whilst Igor (Miss) roared and carried on… usually Rez couldn't concentrate long enough and ended up beating the shit out of him.

Now, as Miss Igor sat there looking across the dock at Rez, his thoughts floated away from his duties up into pinky miasmas.

The Judge: "ummm, across the docks, I see the boy and it's a shock that tenderly I must sentence him".

The Judge tittered to himself and the titter slid down his shirt collar – making love poetry at this time of the day, how terribly risqué! The Judge couldn't keep his thoughts away from worshipping Rez.

The Judge swooned: "He stands there smouldering, cracked smile, sparks of iridescent light in his boyish eyes, brooding a gloom… sombre in this light… he sweats upon my word… he dominates the room like some symbol. A feather? A human heart? I almost feel the presence of supernatural powers… you could see him subtly influence his surroundings. Oh look, his eyelids droop, his genitals sleep…"

The Judge bashes his hammer so hard (fruity glint in his eye) that he comes in his pants (the thing in his pants resembled a floppy bag with a nozzle, the kind of thing you use to ice a cake… an icing bag). Was the Judge guilty of hypocrisy? If I had to pass sentence on him I'd say he was as guilty as hell – but would add that there is no such thing as justice, no such thing as equality, no such thing as law.

Miss Igor had her fun and, because she had to pay for it on many occasions, now she made Rez pay for it, by committing him to ice, to float on a ship without knowing where it was going.

Rez is in the holding room surrounded by four grey walls, awaiting transportation to the ship, and to ice.

Rez, sullen and bored, wants to do a new crime, something he hasn't tried before. Thieving and prostitution were not crimes to brag about – to whom would he brag?

Rez wanted to achieve some kind of notoriety and the only crime that would do it was murder. To murder someone set you apart from the rest of the crowd, it elevated you to lofty heights. He was more than a little deluded.

Nevertheless, he set a crime fantasy in motion in his mind, his violet eyes had that weird unfocussed look – as though he were looking straight through you – his thoughts fixed on one idea.

The murder of a little boy. The murder of little boys, especially by another boy, was all the rage at the moment – it intrigued and outraged the public. It always made international headlines. Rez needed a motive. One instantly came to him – like a child's pop-up book, depicting a woodland scene where a woodsman chopping wood whistles merrily, red and white spotted toadstools gleam, a little boy wearing blue shorts skips happily... the first little boy he sees wearing blue shorts will be the victim. Rez hated that colour, the colour of his mad mother's eyes, the colour of the judge's prick, his father's breath, blue; the colour of the ice, blue; the colour of the sea.

Rez: "I want to kill a little boy in blue shorts, I'll wear black, I'll be an angel of death."

Rez found a sudden meaning to his life. He was going to kill a boy – well, he was going to fantasise about it first. The fantasy would be like a rehearsal.

Rez focuses on the journey out of his childhood, his route to self-destruction. To destroy someone else – the little boy in blue shorts – would be like destroying part of himself, the boy in him. Rez is deep in the trauma zone between what he feels and what he doesn't – a life of erections and broken dreams.

The murder 'rehearsal' falls together like this:

A pair of rusty secateurs discarded in the gutter, needing lubrication – Rez masturbates onto the flaky pincers, images... blue woollen shorts cut, jagged metal catching young boy's thigh, piercing a hole near the boy's scrotum. Rez doesn't picture a face, only tops of legs and lumps where balls should hang. He snarls as he comes, anointing the secateurs with his pearly sperm.

Rez sees the secateurs flying through the air, diving like a Kamikaze plane, glinting in the afternoon sun... the secateurs, like hungry jaws, snap open and gorge into the little boy's eyes, turning anti-clockwise, cutting them out – robbing him of sight, bloody black pits, accompanied by piercing screams. Next the secateurs do their work on blubbering lips, shredding them to crimson ribbons. Blind and dumb now, the instruments of torture snap and bite – lacerating the boy's ears so that his entire face is a bleeding mass of holes, only the nose remains – a geyser of blood.

In the guise of tailor's scissors, the secateurs perforate the kid's stomach, scoring the skin into pleats, so his intestines peek-a-boo from behind their venetian blinds of flesh.

"He's a doll, a paper doll," Rez considers.

Without lips, and from one of the many holes in the little boy, a cartoon bubble pops out. "Why kill me?", it reads.

"You're mine, I can do anything I want with you," Rez screams until he blacks out.

In the black-out, a dead dream, a dream that has the appearance of a non-dream, in this space, Rez dreams up a manifesto about killing and death – or rather I write one for him. I'll write as though de Sade were my guide, his ectoplasmic fingers hover over mine. Rez's manifesto of killing and death:

"Nobody is worth anything, so kill everybody. The world is shit. The juiciest crime is betrayal, find a cause, fight for it, then betray it... all humans are just meat... do unto others as they would do unto you, only do it first, that's the number one rule in killing... killing is beautiful, a final statement, a full stop... killing anyone can make you famous. Killing is an obsession, a passion, the breaker of boundaries, it brings dark where there was light, fear where there was hope, hate where there was love... night, stars, falling in a shower of black sputum, crows screeching a funeral anthem... Hail master! Angel of death, wings of black patent beat behind a torso of bronze, a broken statue moves, powerful arms outstretched welcoming in the latest gathering... Angel of death sweeps up the carnage from the gutters, back-alleyways, battlefields, prisons, dank cellars, tenement blocks: the collector of bullets, the counter of wounds."

Rez, in the dead dream, is metaphorically giving me the thumbs up. He see the images I'm creating on his behalf...

"The Angel of Death leads the corpses and their fleeing spirits to death, master of the unseen, who peels away the flesh and grinds down the bone, sending their souls off to the grand master himself – Old Father Time.

To kill someone is to introduce them to the Angel of Death, the ambassador to Death. The killer is always a servant, a mad dreaming enabler. So death creeps in through every pore, every orifice, slipping into pungent arseholes, hurtling through the bowels masquerading as Aids or cancer… see death waste away your bones with a flip of the wrist. See death pull the plug on your heart, command blood to attack and crash in the brain. Death as a long tube sucking foetuses out of wombs. Behind every atrocity, death sits with his feet up reading a newspaper, waiting, waiting."

Characteristically, the phantom of de Sade grew fidgety and bored, and decided I was on my own.

Rez was stirring from his dead dream-space with the seeds of a new plan of action.

Chapter 5

REZ WOKE AND CHRISTENED HIS AWAKENING BY HACKING UP A GOB of silver phlegm and spurting it into the gutter, where it lay like a fallen meteorite. With a sweep of his beefy knuckles Rez wiped away, along with a saliva bubble, the 'thought rehearsal' of killing a little boy in blue shorts.

He lit a cigarette butt and scanned across the street – an orange neon sign sputtered on and off: "Wrinkles", it flashed. Rez had another inspiration, maybe he could snuff out someone old and grotesque in Wrinkles Bar – an Elephants graveyard.

He stepped off the pavement, crossing the meteorite of spit, which twinkled, and ambled over the road and into the bar... blue screen...

A rather bald mirror-ball turned in slow motion, lighting, from one moment to the next, the dreary clientele, which comprised of geriatric queens and dykes, pan- and tran-sexuals. Usually anyone under fifty wasn't allowed but Rez drifted in. There was a collective gasp at the smell of young flesh... but nobody batted a clogged eyelash, the herd was too busy slurping its favourite beverage – a rather cheap vodka distilled from car antifreeze.

The bar itself was a long plank of wood. Sawdust mixed with glitter was strewn across the floor. A sad string of fairy lights was draped around a mirrored wall – the place looked like an empty circus ring swirling towards the end of time.

Barry Manilow's "I Write The Songs" played at varying speeds on the antiquated juke box.

Rez snuck over to the mirrored wall, his gaze drawn towards a figure standing slightly to one side of the bar. Legs astride, arms dangling by her sides, dressed in a dirty white mini-skirt and matching jacket made of Latex. Lardy legs stuffed into white stilettos, skin puffy pink, long orange hair with bangs shielded her eyes. She stared at Rez. Rez was suspicious, yet at the same time drawn in by some queer allure. He did something he didn't normally do: he smiled. The smile nearly fused the place, it fairly bounced off the walls, showering the clientele in rose petals and pigs ears.

In the time it took for Rez to blink, Ms Thing had teleported over and was now standing right in front of Rez's eyes. A vision to behold.

His eyes were on sting.

Her eyes were on stung.

"So young," said Ms Thing in a strong baritone.

Rez answered by spitting on the floor.

"Young and spunky," Ms Thing declared, transfixed by the lump of spit.

Rez notices that one of Ms Thing's weird pinky eyes is asquint, pointing inwards, so she looks as though she's looking at the tip of her puggish nose.

"You look good enough to eat, young master, like an orchard full of plums, ripe figs, dates, dewberries, lush honey aswarm with bees, O Master, wilt thou come with me?" Ms Thing groaned, all Marlowevian.

Rez expertly held in a snigger.

Ms Thing seemed to be on one...

"You're a boy now, but one day you'll be a man, a twigger, a breeder – a blushing pumping machine... once my trench was a gurgling brook, but now all is withering, my sinews dry... I'd love to..." Ms Thing trails off, her eyes scanning down Rez's chunky frame.

Rez is fascinated by Ms Thing and decides she would be a suitable candidate for a snuffing. He barely had time to finish this thought, when Ms Thing started off on a new tangent, smacking her lips of pearly blue...

"Caviar, Champagne, chocolate, prunes, oysters, espresso, when consumed together make for a rumbling in the belly, and ignite fabulous gasses that explode into fantastic thunderous farts... which prepares the way for the main course." Ms Thing paused. Rez's brows knitted together, his head spinning from the recipe, he couldn't help gazing down upon Ms Thing's cleavage peeking between her open jacket – the 'pillows' looked as though they were made out of two rugby balls, they didn't move.

Rez caught himself staring and asked Ms Thing to buy him a drink.

"In a while dear boy, I want to tell you of my passion, after indulging in the feast of nice things, I like nothing more than to have some handsome boy watch me..." And here she leaned in so close to Rez, that he thought her face would fall into his.

"So young, young, so very young, how old are you by the way?" she asked.

"Um, sixteen," Rez lied, adding on a year.

"Nearly too old, however, I like some beauty to sit and watch me defecate on one of my especially fine china dinner plates and, Oh! yummy, yummy, dine on my very finest turd of turds." Ms Thing concluded, drooling like a sick farm animal.

Ms Thing tottered off to the bar to get their drinks. Rez looked around the club, as one would look around a Museum. Feigning interest, he saw The Thing at the bar fiddle with her bra-strap and pay for the drinks. He looked at his reflection in the mirror, no meaning. Then staring deeper into the looking glass, through a swirl of purple mist, a tableaux from the bar's past unfolds. The images Rez sees at first are in black and white then, the more he concentrates, they bloom into colour – a carnival of porn. He sees women trussed and bound. A bunch of men, mostly sailors, are filling them up with dildos, telephone receivers, knives, guns... close-up of a needle inserted into the eye of a nipple.

Sex scenes unfurl in a riot of combinations: sex with pigs, sex with eels, sex with midgets, amputees – a stump dripping in semen fucking a cunt, then an arse... a group of men stand around a boy

Rez's age, younger perhaps, he is bound and gagged, bent over, wrists tied to ankles, while the men with their fingers, fists, cocks are humping every available orifice... snap of bones, rip of flesh – the scene explodes.

The mirror cracks – segmenting Rez's face, shattering the vision and casting him as a neon angel. He returns to the present and Ms Thing is standing before him, clinking drinks.

"Would you entertain the idea, young master, of accompanying me to my abode, this place is getting on my nerves somewhat," says Ms Thing still in her Marlowevian phase.

"Sure," Rez replies thinking somewhat dimly that it's going to be easier than he imagined – get back to the old bitch's place and then WHAM! cosh her with some blunt instrument.

They down their drinks in one gulp, keeping a frosty eye on each other.

"I would like to take a horse-drawn carriage, but alas, alack, not in this day and age – let's get a taxi," suggests the pretentious old bag. Rez with his hands in his pockets guarding his packet follows Ms Thing out of Wrinkles.

Rez was remembering a story told to him by one of the street boys, a kid had told him about some weird murder... here's the story:

"I was working as a cleaner for a rich Doctor, well he said he was a Doctor, who experimented on bodies... I had to come every day at five and basically sweep and wash his 'operating room' in the basement of his apartment... he picked me up one day outside the Stoly metro station, at first I thought he wanted sex, but he said he wanted to offer me legitimate work, he wanted to help a poor street urchin, something like that, I thought it was a line... but as soon as I arrived at his place he thrust a broom and bucket in my hands and told me to go the basement and clean it up... I was thinking it was one of his pervs or kinks. I went to the basement and *FUCK!* the place was littered with bits of bodies: tits, cocks, tubs full of guts, heads without noses, heads with seven or eight noses, a whole bidet full of ears... fucking creepy... I spewed. So I got some hot water and did as the Doc said. I cleaned. When I'd finished the Doc paid me eighty roubles and said I should come back the next day and do the same, and to keep my trap shut otherwise I'd end up in the basement with the rest of the dead meat. I said I would do as he asked, even though he gave me the willies. He had this one eye, glass, sort of dull blue with a film over it... but eighty roubles a day was an offer I couldn't refuse, it meant I could stop selling my arse.

So I go there every day for a month and I'm getting very rich, but all those dead bits of meat are really getting to me. I'm cleaning up the blood, veins, bits of rotting muscle, and the Doc is watching me with his one beady eye.

This one day I'm cleaning and the Doc is watching me and I don't know what happened but I turned around and screamed 'What the fuck are you looking at?' And the Doc replied, 'My next experiment.'

I pissed myself and the Doc started laughing, a horrible laugh, like a witch, his dead eye with its veil glued on me... I just couldn't take it anymore. I picked up the broom, and before I knew what I'd

done, I'd thrust the end of the broom right into that hideous eye –
oddly enough it fitted the socket really well. The old Doc screamed
as the broom handle disappeared right to the back of his skull and
sort of stopped with a *thud!* He thrashed about the room with the
entire broom sticking out of the socket – blood spraying everywhere.
I laughed because the whole thing looked so funny. He twirled about
bashing into things screaming 'Clean this mess up'.

I gave the broom one more shove and watched it come out of
the back of the old fucker's head, splattering his nasty brains
asunder. He crashed to the floor with the broom still upright. I did
a little dance, burgled the place – selling the body parts as fresh
meat to the butchers on Smirnoff Avenue."

Chapter 6

A T THE HOUSE OF MONSTROSITY WHERE MS THING LIVED. TO SAY that it looked like an elbow pointing at the sky, covered in Ivy, would be quite accurate. A Gothic tenement, sixteen stories high. The building was complete with curly spires and top hat chimney pots, upon which perched huge crows and ravens, the occasional vampire bat swooped. A place of shadows.

Ms Thing's apartment was one big room sectioned off by screens, sparsely furnished with one bed and a dressing table with fairy lights and a faded mirror – it was in fact a cosier version of Wrinkles. A collection of stuffed crocodiles of all sizes lay head to tail along one of the walls, their dead eyes glinting with untold secrets and forbidding north winds. Shoes, bras, commingle with rotting cheese and nail polish, all coated in thick dust. In short, the place was a dump.

Ms Thing took off her jacket and Rez couldn't help notice that her tits were really rugby balls slung into a bra.

"I want to fuck! I'll fuck anything, animal, vegetable, mineral," said Ms Thing, hitching up her skirt way above her flabby thighs. Rez sat on the edge of the bed and to his surprise (and mine) got a hard-on. Ms Thing revealed more (no panties) and the fact she wasn't made like other women, for she had what they didn't have, but she wished she had what she lacked...

She was cuntless. A cock dangled down from a pubic bush of ginger hair – no balls. Head thrown back now, caution to the wind, she twirled around making a screeching noise as though she were about to reveal the seventh wonder of the world, but didn't give a fuck. Rez just stared.

Now Ms Thing, pure brazen hussy, wobbled forward and waved her love knot right in Rez's face and do you know what, Rez betrayed himself, he came in his pants.

Ms Thing took control of the situation, she saw the stain appear in his pants and swooped down ripping open the flies and pulling out his wet cock, began lapping up the love juice – this was such a shock – Ms Thing has literally made it explode in our faces.

Rez's lower regions felt like soggy trifle. He felt all at sea. Ms Thing drained him dry, then he forcefully pushed her head off his lap and shoved her onto the floor. Maybe this was the moment?

"My, my, guttersnipe, a bit of rough play," jested Ms Thing, flicking her hair back behind her ears trying to look seductive but looking more and more like a rugby player in drag. Rez buttoned up his trousers and held out his hand. He assumed he was going to get paid.

Ms Thing looked at this gesture and decided to play along.

"Yes you have nice hands," she said.

Rez, in this sleazy nightmare, was enchanted by Ms Thing's strange allure. Something shifted, reality hit him hard in the face,

Ms Thing exuding misty veils of Maya. He got straight to the point. "Give me sixty roubles," he was a boy of few words but enjoyed conjuring images and imaginary landscapes. He could see Ms Thing now up to her neck in burning hot sand as the vultures and buzzards circled and dashed and dined on her face, the long stringy plucking-out of eyes...

"Roubles? Roubles? What do you want sixty roubles for?" Ms Thing demanded to know – she was puffy, ankle deep into her game.

Rez's eyes narrowed, he puffed up, nearly filling up the room, he looked around for a blunt instrument. But there was only a broken hairdryer and the wall of Crocodiles.

Rez felt dumb and shattered, he couldn't reconcile what had happened. He wanted payment.

"Can you give me forty roubles?" Rez asked, trying a different tactic, what he knew as charm – he smiled – something shifted, the room got hotter... Ms Thing lay with her head on one of the crocodiles

"I will give you all you need, everything you know and dream but you must cross the line," She *gesprecksang* cryptically.

Rez turned to stone. Ms Thing shivered and squirmed with lust. Rez as Master.

She reiterated her song.

"I will give you all you read and need, but you must cross the line."

Life was ever strange for Rez, a weird game, and so with no blunt instrument in sight – he crossed the line.

*

We pause on Rez for a moment to take a look at Ms Thing's his-story:

Born Ivor Ruskcrumbinski in St Petersburg about fifty years ago, ex-army sergeant, acquired a taste for boys, drugs and ca-ca whilst invading Poland during the war. Show biz pretensions, owned a flea circus before joining the army, but became so bitten and infected from the bites he had to sack his employees (the fleas) saying that you can't have people (fleas) working for you if they have vicious intentions.

Ivor spent years wandering lost in Psyberia, looking for a meaning to life. Eventually while staying on a farm, he met and courted a milk maid called Babska. Her parents were against the liasion from the very beginning – perhaps it was because Ivor wore Babs' pinafore dresses (oddly enough this didn't seem to bother Babs). The couple eloped to Moscow where things took a turn for the worse. It was at this time that Ivor, due to circumstances beyond his control and following his natural urges, began frequenting the few gay bars there were in Moscow while poor Babs pined away in their little attic room. To the emerging Ms Thing, Babs was becoming a vague memory, a daughter even. It was sad, sad, sad.

Suddenly one day Babs keeled over and died from neglect. One dies and one is born. Babs died, Ms Thing was born.

Ms Thing inherited Babs' wardrobe, which was dire and naff in the extreme, flower print blouses, rough sacking cape smelling of rats' piss, wooden boots – the 'Haute Peasant' look – not the kind of drag to swish around the nightclubs in. To get the cash for a new wardrobe Ms Thing went to work in a brothel – she became known for her wily tongue.

Before I get bogged down in detail and strip Ms Thing of any potential mystery or glamour I must emphasise that she is a tragic object, and possibly fascinating. She must be allowed to bask in the shadows... to 'explain' her or reduce her to merely a cipher would not be kind at all – for Rez she is a catalyst, his spiritual redeemer.

Part 2

"Shopping"

Dada wouldn't buy me a Bow-Wow

Chapter 7

"WHAT'S A BIRD TOO BIG FOR ITS NEST? SIX LETTERS." REZ asks Ms Thing who looks utterly nonplussed, and answers "Emu".

"No, that's only three letters." Rez counts on his fingers. "It could be Thrush," he muses – Ms Thing looks down at her lap. She interjects with an inspired, "F-L-A-M-I-N-G-O."

"No," Rez grumbles. "Natasha digs a ditch, three letters then six?"

Rez is confused and irritable, doing the daily crossword in the Moscow Tribune, one of the many daily rituals he and Ms Thing do together. They had come to an arrangement since that first night three months ago. It was a simple one, sex and companionship in exchange for pocket money and a roof over his head – Ms Thing, the sugar mummy. Rez's mad mother had been committed to a Psyberian insane asylum but it was only a rumour. The rumour blew in through an open window in a shallow whisper that froze his ears, the angelic trumpets of his imagination.

So they had set up a 'relationship' without my permission. They lived by that maxim that Madonna spoke of in one of her songs. 'The pursuit of pleasure should not depend on the permission of another'. HUMPF! Surely it's more a case of 'You scratch my back and I'll scratch yours.'

Rez and Ms Thing created their own realm. Ms Thing focused all her waking attention on him, so the place was pretty sordid. Funny smells like boot polish and rotting eggs emanated from under the bed. The bed where their strange and intimate couplings took place – I don't know if I can bring myself to describe in detail their... sex life...

Although 'it' repulsed him the fuck would go something like this:

Ms Thing in the doggie position, her orange mane and face pushed into red velveteen pillows, her geriatric anus pointing to the ceiling, like a Pantomine Horse or Surrealist chair.

Rez would close his beautiful violet eyes and enter the realm of his imagination, conjuring up all sorts of horrors and perversions to get a hard-on.

At nearly sixteen he was indeed a 'Big Boy', in truth his cock was approximately nine inches by six – extremely solid and powerful, it rose majestically – a Dinosaur waking.

His eyes closed tight and his jeans wrapped around his ankles. He shuffled towards Ms Thing's ancient arsehole whose lips, once puckered, now wilted like a dying flower (without wishing to be too cruel) it now looked something akin to the mouth of a headless pig, with all the accompanying odours.

It would be easy to pity Rez at this moment but, to be frank, this boy had a wayward side, he saw the act of fucking Ms Thing as investigative work, he used his magnificent tool – the tool of his trade – as an instrument of excavation. In entering Ms Thing, he was entering another world, dank, slushy, fathomless. He was in some way fucking death.

Ms Thing was nearer to death, she was on a slow suicide into death. The act of fucking her represented a dark destiny for Rez.

His cock penetrated Ms Thing's cavern, filling it up, extinguishing all light, he never held her love handles, he let his tool find its own way in. It was a good job his tool was so large, if not it would have felt as though he was falling into teeming bilge.

Once inside, Ms Thing gave a gruff little whimper – then they were locked, her face eclipsed by the red velveteen pillows.

Her vision became microscopic, so that particles of dust took on the appearance of valleys of weird creatures. What I mean is, micro became macro and macro became micro... Her perception, due to Rez's fucking, became god-like. He plugged her into hyperreality, pushed her into a new space. Their coupling at once hideous and transgressive.

I think some light relief, some image of beauty should be interposed here. Perhaps moonlight flooding through stained glass windows, casting kaleidoscopic colours across their fucking. Rez kneeling behind Ms Thing, his perfectly smooth white body defined by shadows, every muscle highlighted by the moonlight. His flat nipples like glowing mandalas, body arched back, a Brancusi curve... and that cock – eel in a cave – blond crop haloed by candlelight, eyes closed so tight, lips bitten and swollen on the periphery of pleasure?

About twenty or so brutal rammings inside of Ms Thing and Rez would get the pre-climax shudders, the feeling of piercing membrane, his helmet the mushroom cloud of a nuclear explosion. He puffs up as Ms Thing thrashes about braying like a donkey.

The inside of Ms Thing's baggy butt impregnated by Rez's blinding, celestial white light, his jissom, the milky way, giving birth to new planets. Rez has, as they say, put some life back in the old thing. Ms Thing, the cosmic sex vampire feeding on his youthful fluids and energies, lies prostrate on the bed like rotting fruit.

Rez looked down at his wilting cock as it once more curled and shrunk back to sleep until the next time...

If we could see inside of Ms Thing's bowels, they would look like this... glittering phospherescent dome, a cave where man first found fire. A gurgling, swirling mess of infinite illuminations... squelchy inundations.

Ms Thing cleared her throat and farted an unmentionable substance onto the bed.

"There are several things that draw us together, most terribly our silence." She was regurgitating, practically word for word, what the writer Anais Nin had said to French loony Antonin Artaud.

Rez looked at the beached whale aloft the bed, then gazed down at his deflowered proboscis and mumbled...

"I want a pet, a dog, cat, bird, pig."

Ms Thing, in a good but weird mood, replied,

"Anything your startling heart desires, my dear, what sort of pet do you want?"

"Something queer, something odd," he said pouting.

"I think I know just the place," she said.

They took a cab.

Ms Thing, luckily for her, had become very wealthy by trading in foreign currency – also bits of crap, ephemera to rich Italian and American tourists. She recently sold a 1947 biscuit tin, hewn from a Russian tank. She sold the piece of junk as art to a wealthy American artist, who wallowed in kitsch – had made an international career out of it. Ms Thing had sold it, and herself along with it, for a reported 7,000,000 roubles – enough for her and Rez to live on indefinitely.

Chapter 8

THE CAB HURTLED DOWN AND AROUND MOSCOW'S SIDE STREETS, across Red Square, over a bridge and pulled up outside what looked like a brewery, but on closer inspection was a dilapidated church.

Ms Thing paid the driver and she and Rez got out and stood on the curb.

"A friend of mine lives here," said Ms Thing tweaking Rez's left nipple beneath his 'I'VE SEEN EINSTEIN'S EYES' T-shirt. Watching hot breath fume out of Rez's nostrils, already a young mythic god, Ms Thing adjusts her bra. The pair scramble to the front door.

Ms Thing pursed her lips against the large letter box, carved in the shape of a sea-serpent and cooed:

"Hillo, Countess Handover, it's me" she rapped on the door three times. Rez started at the pitch of Ms Thing's shriek, her voice could pierce a sphincter at forty meters.

The door slowly opens, great wafts of lilac dust intermingle with the flickering light of a movie projector, the door opens wide and there stands the Countess Handover.

The Countess Handover is a vision to behold, standing at nearly six foot five – she looked like someone, God presumably, had scribbled her into existence with a big fat marker pen.

Thick black hair, which could be a wig, sprayed into abeyance by tons of laquer, giving it a superbly unreal effect... her eyes definitely belonged to the dead or extra-terrestrial, for they were black with a purple sheen. Her face, what might once have been described as 'Moony', now only resembled a burnt-out version of that glowing orb... her emaciated frame concealed by a Chanel two-piece. The Countess of doom smiled – bright green teeth – opening her arms to embrace Ms Thing as a Hawk embraces its prey.

"My dear, long see no time," the Countess rasped, getting the phrase hopelessly mixed up and then under her breath in a less gracious tone... "Fuck me with a rusty sardine can, who's the beauty?" Her black eyes fixating on Rez, who shivered not because of the Countess, but because he was still on the front step.

"ENTER," said the Countess, grandly ushering them in. Ms Thing stepped into the hallway, flipping her hair about. Rez ambled forward looking up at the huge chandelier, dripping with candle wax – the fixture was made entirely from Elephant trunks. The effect was stunning in a funny peculiar way, for it seemed to Rez that all the dead Elephants had runny noses. He sniggered.

Ms Thing and the Countess ignored the snigger. Rez gazed about the hall that was constantly shifting realities, as though it were dissolving. What he thought were doors turned into shadows, what he first saw as lights were stars poking through a roof. A staircase vanished in a puff of smoke.

The Countess penetrated the sudden stilted atmosphere, broke the hymen of silence.

"He doesn't say much does he dear?" she said, pointing a bony finger at Rez.

"He's deep, he's dreamy," defended Ms Thing as though Rez wasn't there.

"He's a pretty thing, *que bella cosa*," replied the Countess, batting her eyelashes that were made of... mink, rat, otter.

"I'd like to purchase a pet for my young friend," Ms Thing piped up.

"What had you in mind – anything?" said the Countess preparing to volley. The two ladies couldn't just girl-talk, there was always an underlying competitiveness that infused their infrequent meetings – they knew too much about each other's pasts to be comfortable.

Put simply, Ms Thing had worked for the Countess in days of yore – as a Courtesan in the Countess's Brothel, the Iron Cervix. In this former incarnation Ms Thing was known as Lady Buttmunch Supremo.

"I'd like something..." Rez spoke, his voice strangely deep and butch. The two hags stared.

"I want a pet," Rez trailed off again, the place was having a peculiar effect on him, as though his sub-conscious were filtering into his conscious mind.

"What he would like, dear Countess, is something to play with," said Ms Thing.

"Something to love!" the Countess cut in, twisting all manner of implications into one sentence. The Countess could still impale one with a phrase.

Suddenly, everything seemed to happen at the last minute, a final moment's notice – a hideous screeching noise like the side of a car being scraped with a nail-file, swooped above the trio's heads... they glanced up, the Countess raising her left eyebrow, giving her a Modigliani countenance...

They saw a creature so very odd... wings of an Eagle, or some other bird of prey, face of a piglet, body of a Lizard, legs from a Sheep. The freaky creature swooped clumsily again and shat, the swampy turd landing with a *thwack!* splattering at Rez's feet. The creature grunted / barked / chirped and disappeared into the vast nothingness.

"Pardon my Vamoose, don't know how that one got out," said the Countess. Ms Thing holding her puggish nose turned away from the abominable stench.

"What was this place," Rez wondered, "was it a dream within a dream?"

The Countess Handover since leaving her profession as Madam, had returned to her former career as a Genetic Engineer, a master of hybrids, mistress of misfits.

The Countess Handover had closed the Iron Cervix after a grand mutiny by the 'girls' back in 1966 – a lot of the girls working began to lose body parts in their sleep, they'd wake to find parts of their bodies lost or grafted onto others. It became completely insane when on one occasion the Countess stitched together a girl with a client – *in coitus*.

The Countess, by way of nervous breakdown, had reverted to her old career... the breakdown caused by an unsuccessful sex change operation – done on the cheap, she was left neither man nor woman – she turned her rage, and some say revenge, onto the animal kingdom, and began experimenting with new types of pets, yet all she succeeded in doing was creating abominations. But she found a market for them – rich shits with demented tastes. It was no longer chic to own a poodle or Mancoon cat, people demanded something new and unique and the Countess delivered.

"Yes, something like that thing," Rez pointed to thin air. Ms Thing and the Countess sighed.

"He wants a thing to love!" hissed the Countess.

"Well, do you have anything then?" Ms Thing finally snapped.

Ms Thing gasped, a terrible pain shot through her body, the Countess and Rez stood back against a wall that wasn't there. Standing behind Ms Thing on its hind legs was a magnificent Black Stallion with its teeth sunk into Ms Thing's shoulder. Ebony mane standing up on end, teeth sinking into Ms Thing's flesh, as though it were made of clay.

Impaled on the spot – her mouth open in a silent scream – the horse and Thing thrash about in petrified slow motion.

Rez notices the horse's prick – foreskin back looking for an entrance – horse ballooning out of shape. One of Ms Thing's rugby ball tits bursts with a thunderous clap – the killer horse from hell simply dematerialised.

"One of my specials, The Phantom Killer Stallion a la hologram," the heinous Countess announced.

"I could've died!" gurgles Ms Thing.

"But you didn't, did you," says the Countess finishing Ms Thing off. "It took me years," she continued, "to perfect that breed years of experimentation, lost a lot of people on the way though, but as you can see, I've worked on it so it appears real, but is, in fact, just a hologram, fooled you didn't it, my dear?"

"What a fucking nightmare, it's not what we're looking for," spat Ms Thing through gritted teeth.

"It doesn't cost much to feed, just bits of old celluloid, it's particularly partial to Marx Brothers movies," the Countess inflected.

Rez was growing despondent amid the slings and arrows of outrageousness – between the two hags.

"I want SOMETHING," Rez cried.

"Oh, my darling boy," yelped Ms Thing picking herself together, rearranging her 'pillows'.

The Countess put her hand over her mouth and tried not to titter at the wreck scraping its self off the floor.

This is how Shakespeare described the two hags:

"What are these, so withered and wild in their attire, they look not like the inhabitants of the earth. And yet are on it? Live you? Or are you aught that man may question? By each at once her choppy finger laying, upon her skinny lip: You should be women and yet your beards forbid me to interpret that you are so."

"Cuntless, do you have anything?" spat The Thing as she looked at Rez, who was so dejected yet sexy. Her heart tried to skip a beat but failed.

"Fear not, Girl Thing, I've just thought of something very precious." With this the Countess swished about and from a shelf above her head – in the middle of nowhere – pulled down a box.

"Oh, darling boy," said Ms Thing.

"If only I had a proper cunt, one as deep as the ocean, then my darling one could plummet its depths, his cock could then take a journey through me... oh, maybe that old bitch could sew us together... he could lap at my monthly fountain of blood, my red red river... oh, if I had real tits, celestial udders, from which the creamiest milk would flow, I could be a fountain of many sources for him... oh, to have a cunt, a cunt of cunts... I want to feel his cock in my cunt talking away, reciting filth, I WANT A CUNT! OH! OH, FOR CUNT-POWER!" Ms Thing's mind nearly caving in from rabid cunt-envy.

"Et voila!" hissed the Countess holding a brown paper box in her talons. "This is so very precious and has the most delicious history to it."

Rez, full of frustrated wonder, asked what was in it.

"A treasure, my little zizi," said the Count, unshamedly flirting, batting her furry eyelashes at him.

Ms Thing, who was on the point of extreme psychosis, snapped: "Open the frigging box!"

"It's not Pandora's, it's Judy's," teased the Countess.

The Countess took the lid off the box. Inside laying in an inch or so of sawdust was a small Teddy bear, tufts of yellow fur, black bead eyes scratched and cracked – black cotton thread for a mouth... from the neck to the end of its body, was cut open cotton stuffing, smeared in blood. A gift card yellowing with age lay beside it... it read: "TO TOM LOVE JUDY".

The Countess lowered the box and showed Rez and an appalled Ms Thing.

"I think this would be suitable, it's expensive, but it doesn't need feeding – you can have many happy hours, just gazing at it," informed the cranky Countess.

"Oh," sighed Rez.

"We'll take it," groaned Ms Thing.

"My dears, do not be disappointed, this little curio belonged to none other than that great American singing legend... Judy Garland!... it was a *momento mori* for one of her lovers, who did her wrong... it's actually her blood smeared on the little bear, and to you only 2,000 roubles."

The Countess closed the lid and handed it over to Rez, her talons accidentally-on-purpose scratched his hand.

"OOH! So sorry, but I do love to leave my mark!" she hissed.

Rez saw tiny droplets of blood rise to the surface, he watched as they disappeared again. Ms Thing and the Countess had gone to war, like two snake's tongues slithering over lips, eyes darting. Rez took the box and went towards the door Ms Thing followed, scattering Roubles as she went.

Rez turned around. The Countess Handover vaporised into multi-coloured smoke. The huge door closing like a chapter in history. A cab pulled up.

Rez turned to Ms Thing and said, "Who was Judy Garland?"

INTERLUDE

Supernatural Boy (I Had a Dream)

REZ AND I ARE DREAMING THE SAME DREAM. REZ AS A WARRIOR BOY of great strength and beauty. A prize catch for any old queen, except no old queen is going to get him. He is mine.

This dream we're dreaming: Rez has been hibernating in heaps of ash, recalling ancient wisdoms. His appearance has changed, to someone of a warmer climate... he has bright green eyes, brown coffee coloured skin, lean, muscled, dark blond hair, body as lithe as an Antelope. Red cod-piece hides a meaty cock.

Rez and I in the dream within the dream: A tornado of porn mags, chains rattling, white mists of sex, fears in the shadows. Two men fall onto a mattress, spitting cobra venom, clenched fists, images breaking up... distant whimpering.

In this dreaming interlude we link, through time and space, we meet in lush grass interiors, our eyes dilated from smoking ash tree bark. I wipe sleep from his eye... I, the mind, he the body – not just the body – his instincts outweigh mine. My blue intellect, his red passion. I don't want to sound like Christopher Isherwood here, eulogising over boys, like some over-educated prissy queen with a prick like a rotting maggot, slithering, slobbering over my

Rez. Some old queen's prick like the neck of a turtle with dead beady eyes on either side, mouth gaping open, drooling pre-cum juice or feeding on a passing fly.

Rez, my beautiful warrior boy, in the dream in this dream: I've gone to pieces, finally gone to pieces, something I've been meaning to do for a long time. These thoughts of Rez being tampered with, in this dream, will send me over the edge. It will want to make me murder any old queen within a five hundred mile radius... an old queen comes into my mind.

REVENGE OF THE KILLER QUEEN

"I take a little silver scalpel and neatly slice the old bitch's maggot prick into segments. Segments that make up the whole. Watch each segment wriggle, trying to put itself back together again. And suddenly it's like I've committed surgery. A neat dissection that looks *so* sweet to me. I wrap the pieces, by this stage; though I would've gone to pieces. I wrap the old cunt's dissected maggot prick (I'm only interested in the prick), I wrap the gory pieces in grey muslin and call them "DESMOND". DESMOND'S pieces. Rez wouldn't see this, but if he asked me what's in that hat box? If he asked me, "What's in that hat box?" I would have to show him DESMOND or DESMOND'S pieces, all neatly dissected and wrapped in the grey muslin – placed carefully at the bottom of the hat box in the deep, voluminous interior of the hat box, silk lining of mustard showing off the grey muslin bundles of DESMOND.

Yes I could easily *dice* a human being. Or any old, revolting, redundant, poor excuse for a skin-graft, malodorous toad, an old queen like DESMOND deserves to have their PIGGIE POKER lopped off.

Let me count the ways:

Removal of his maggot by skewer – take a kebab skewer, red hot – and thrust it down the shaft of his prick, wait for the screaming to stop, about twenty minutes, then push the skewer all the way down so that it gives the floppy flesh pencil, some sort of back bone, so that at least it resembles an erection. Garnish with chilli sauce and there you have it: "DONNA DESMOND".

You see I've become obsessive about Rez, about his protection, his exquisite beauty, which I create and therefore is mine. He is the jewel in my mind. Human perfection.

Stars in their final twinkle blink at our perishing rendezvous. The body may decay but, like Dorian Gray, I project an image onto Rez of me at sixteen, thin, pale, ethereal, girlie, a tiny flower waiting for a 'Rez' to pollinate me with his silky dust. We drink poison from ash tree bark.

The dream changes:

I stand perforated by an abstract moonlight in a tarry swamp, ash tree roots transfigure into huge snakes, purple and bloated with a new kill. All is dark. I watch a single star burn out. Through dead trees I see a flash of bright green. Rez's eyes like fireflies ignite the night. I can feel the satin texture of his skin, before he comes near. Some other freak comes in, someone who wants to interfere. This time it's an old wizard, well not actually a real wizard, more a middle-aged, ex-hippy, speed freak, psychic fascist called *Wizend*.

A wrinkled hyena-faced old geezer with a couple of rotting teeth in his exploding head, which is crammed full of warped cosmic concepts rattling about, making a terrible, and terribly boring, din.

Old Wizened stands, his nobbly knees deep in swamp, pointing an accusative finger at me, wagging and waving it like a divining rod – except old Wizened is powerless, he's a fake, his mind burnt out long ago through snorting tons of Amphetamine Sulphate (the speed has also withered his 'magic wand' to the size of a splinter) and now he's interrupting my, our, dream with his gestures, he's trying to tell me I am consumed by *Dark Forces* – oh yawn, he points to a mouse-grey sky, which cracks open and I wait for some revelation but nothing happens.

I tell old Wiz, "It's just a rip in reality, you stupid old fucker, not one of your prophecies coming down on me, you has-been that hasn't-been-yet!"

Poor old Wiz suddenly feels his own powerlessness, he hides his vulture-like visage deep in the orange hood of his robe. Giving off a scent of fear and stolen goods.

Rez hides behind a tree, its charred skeleton only partially conceals him. Old Wiz stands naked, an awful sight like a crumpled paper bag – quivering and ashamed...

"I peel you away," say I.

And as though I were ripping up newspaper, I rip and tear his image, scattering it far and wide into the stinking swamp.

Rez comes out from behind the dead tree, he smiles and the dark sky turns white. I close my eyes, feeling his breath on my neck and I want to gush forth with proclamations of love and desire, but we are without language. We must reinvent not only language but also ourselves.

Beneath our skin our cells are colliding, mirroring a bond out of time. To love his image, to desire so violently the indefinable quality of his being. Rez, this dream, dream of dreams, he orbits me as though I'm a planet and he's not sure where to land. We are seeking to find a moment so we can fuse together. Blazing shards of morning sunlight spill through the blinds. The sleeper awakens.

Part 3

"Collapse"

Give me sodomy or give me death

— Diamanda Galas

Little red sports car

Fate is uninsurable: The little red sports car skids in the abstract. Smell of burning rubber. Some movie star loses an earring. Impact hits the screen, passing palm trees nodding in the cool breeze in sleepy obedience to the smog; Impact hits the screen, shattering it into a thousand diamonds. Foot slams, brakes jam, the yellow lines wave goodbye to the straight and narrow, diving into virtual smithereens. U-turn his head around your dick, gears shift and a hollow moon turns red neon under the instructions of artifice. Your hips against his lips, spews burning gasoline up into your arsehole, holy halo of fire.

Diamanda Galas screams from the car stereo, "Do you take this Man?" Hands off, the bumper grinds, hood throbs, wheel turns like the skeleton of a burnt out planet, steered by some phantom chauffeur from a former pile up – blood, sperm and glass commingle in this Jackson Pollock of collisions. Reduced to bleeding rag dolls in sorrowful emulation of Jayne Mansfield's last ride.

Chapter 9

The Beginning of the End

NOW TO STEAL A LOOK AT THE PAGES OF MS THING'S JOURNAL, A pretentious little tome in which she records her daily ponderings. Her spidery scrawl dashes across the blue coloured paper in red ink, from a vicious quill – spiraling paragraphs that vibrate with a peculiar poignancy. The journal is her secret text – that she in her addled mind imagines publishing one day – on the twelfth of never, perhaps?

Her pages...

"I've been thinking, how can I not think about my age. I have to face the fact I'm getting on... I shall recline into a sulky attitude. Yet my pleasure is to endlessly ponder. If I'm not thinking about the vast computations of sexual excess with Rez... there I go again. I can't seem to get past my delusions, my whole life is delusion heaped upon delusion, illusion upon delusion... I am the great deluded one, Santa Delusia... If I keep this up there will soon be an explosion of madness, my text, my journal, my life, will fall into a facile nothingness, propelling my psyche towards death."

Here Ms Thing trailed off for a moment and put down her quill that was now drier than a nun's cunt and looked at her hands.

The hands of a labourer, fingernails daubed in yucky pink varnish, ginger hair covering the backs of them, where she had neglected to shave them.

'I am a monstrosity,' she thought.

To divert herself once more she dipped her quill in the red ink, her life's blood, and was about to put quill to paper, when out of the corner of her eye, she saw Rez sleeping on the floor.

The teddy bear Ms Thing had bought him was slung in the corner. Rez had taken a couple of Nembutal sleeping pills to snuff out the boredom. Ms Thing was literally boring him to death. She aimed and tilted her quill and spilled her guts out.

"He's my little Antigone, his tender neck like a poem, he's my executioner of love, my dark angel boy."

Ms Thing sighed and one solitary tear slid down her craggy face. She returned to the sanctuary of her text. She worked through her self-hate with the aid of a quill.

"My childhood," she went on, "was a trauma that sent my soul into confusion (the significance of pedarastic love). Rez the beloved, who will have no other fate than my love. Rez the beloved becomes the object ordained to represent death. This is his beauty and when I die, when I do, he will be even more handsome. I will commission him through my death to live in my stead, my heir apparent. He doesn't love me, he reproduces me. But I'm killing him off by boring him to death."

The red ink ran out again – she stopped.

She knew she had begun to write out her own death. She would finish the game so that Rez, her beloved of beloveds could truly begin his life. A sacrifice so supreme that she believed she would become a martyr, immortalised in literature, film and stage.

Ms Thing felt two things simultaneously – despair and elation. She looked over to Rez, his eyelashes fluttering in his sleep, a little rivulet of dribble running down his bum-fluff chin. Perfection.

Oh, Ms Thing, you are sad and deluded. I almost want to say that I love you, but I don't, it would be a lie, you're repulsive. In an extract from Ms Thing's journal we find out about a dream concerning her twin brother:

"I dreamt of my twin last night, I dreamt that I killed him. He had an illness. He was a monk in the dream, in a long flowing cassock. He was suffering. He was silent. He was ill because he stuck to his vows and because he wanted to change the colour of his skin to that of an Arab man and fuck me. I wanted him to fuck me (keep it in the family) but it didn't seem likely and it made me sick and it made me want to kill him.

In fact, he was haunted by his lust for me – his twin brother. In the dream I appeared as a man, which was extremely distressing. I told him I would sleep with anyone for the right price. He had taken a vow of silence, the stinking ecclesiastical pig. I called him a hypocrite. I yelled in his sweaty face, that like a succubus I'd get him in his sleep. He lit a candle to ignite his misery. He appeared as a monument to anguish. My twin, the virgin. His cock had never fucked a cunt or arsehole, it had never been christened with a ring of shit.

His 'cherry' had never been stretched. Wanking was sin *numero uno*. He starts babbling the lord's prayer, but I note that he's reciting backwards in a fiery red tongue. Then he accuses me of enticing Lucifer into his life. My twin is attached to the church and god by umbilical chord. 'THE LOVE OF GOD IS THE MOST DECEPTIVE LOVE OF ALL,' I say. He falls to his knees. He becomes a knot. He says to me: 'IT IS THE INFINITE MERCY OF THE LORD.'

I tell him he is a fool and that his only accomplishment is breaking a communion wafer in half.

Three witches meet on red velvet seats, swallowing Mandrax like sacred wafers, writing in the black air... their curses.

When I looked at my twin again, he was laying on a slag heap disfigured by long grass and dead flowers...

'Are you dead?' I asked. The wind blew in howling gusts.

'I will become a martyr,' he replied and died.

At the top of the tower, I held my twin's lifeless body in my arms... I loosened his cassock and ran my frozen hands down his lean torso, making the sign of the cross over his face, the smile of the Virgin Mary... who my twin was now fucking up the arse in heaven...

Even in her dreams now, her death was making itself present. Rez, as I have said, entered a kind of coma period.

He had turned into a creature of sensations – a hedonist. Sex, drugs, dreams were his daily fare. He was in danger though of disappearing from himself. Ms Thing had found a new meaning, which was no meaning other than death.

Rez had lost meaning. He was already gone.

The change in Ms Thing was glacial. This feeling for death became like gangrene in her mind. She flitted between Rez's needs and her own secret desire, that was beginning to transcend death. To see the extent of her misery is to read her epic poem, *A Hole Never To Be Found*. She wrote it in blood. Her quill was vampiric.

A Hole Never To Be Found:
'I am the Sphinx, the abyss within, I am my own plague... I want to write beyond my destiny... I look at my feet, they're swollen, now lying in a wheat field weeping, the air thick with curses... my mother cut me out like a cut out doll, had me dressed in paper dresses of A4 and then ripped me up and tossed me out. There is always some part of me that keeps an eye on sadness... THERE IS NO OTHER SOURCE OF BEAUTY THAN THE WOUND... and I have a hole that will never be found... this is the source of my wound.'

The page on which the poem was written was saturated with blood, sweat and tears.

Ms Thing felt so bad, she woke Rez up from his drugged sleep and wanked him off, catching his sperm in a little jar, which she later used as cold creme. Sometimes he came directly onto her face – from the 'tap' as she called it.

Rez felt like a veal calf. Numb in the nether regions of the Nembutals. With her face now taut with his love-juice, Ms Thing dashed out to the Pharmacy to renew her supply of pills.

Rez, alone, tried to pull himself together. Propped up beside one of the crocodiles he looked down the length of his supine body... his feet seemed further away... his thighs looked more curvaceous. His thoughts deep in fog about Ms Thing, certainly he was bored servicing the old hag, but he was so blasé now, he took it with a pinch of salt (lint? dust?). He wondered if there wasn't more to life than being the captive object of adoration. He was waiting for something to happen.

Ms Thing, at the Pharmacy counter, handed over her 'script' for 200 Nembutals. The 'Dolls' as Jackie Susann had once called them. Ms Thing had seen Ms Susann at a book signing back in the early 70s in St Petersburg, when the writer was promoting her third novel *The Love Machine*. She signed Ms Thing's book, giving her a queer look (Ms Thing was still in her 'Haute Peasant' phase). Ms Thing adored Ms Susann, loved her taste in clothes, the psychedelic Pucci pants suits, the Eygptian ankh pendant slung casually around her neck. "An original," thought Ms Thing at the time. Little did she know that the writer Truman Capote had described her as "a truck driver in drag".

The pharmacist also gave Ms Thing a funny look but handed over the bottles of Nembies. Most people, it had to be said, gave her queer looks, it was nothing new, she stared up at a blinking neon light.

Rez staggered over to the window, opening it to the late afternoon sunlight. In the distance the red and gold domes of Moscow glinted, star-bursting in his eyes. He sighed. Little droplets of melancholia trickled through him. There he was, up in that weird ivy tower, looking down on the streets where he once lived. He daydreamed that if he just leapt out, he'd be back to where he started – and Ms Thing would be just a lost corner of Psyberspace, a disjunctive dream.

"Who am I? Where do I really come from? I am Rez and I say this because I know how to say this. Maybe I'll burst into little pieces and remake myself into ten thousand aspects of fame."

Ms Thing in a cab riding homeward: the cab moving at a snail's pace through a thickening fog that depresses her. To cheer herself up she shakes her handbag and the percussive rattle of pills reassures her that in death she'll eat cock and ca-ca.

Rez sat watching TV, channel hopping. Ms Thing had installed cable – a movie channel – 'Red Star' which showed foreign films. The opening title on the screen, Rez mouthed the words T.H.E.O.R.E.M. by Pier Paulo Pasolini. Starring Terence Stamp.

In silence Silvana Mangano crosses herself, she is wearing a preposterous wig that resembles a plastic bloom. Stamp lounges, in the garden – leaves blow on his lap, the maid tries to brush them off – Rez sees a close up of Stamp's packet.

The maid rushes through a sterile white kitchen to look in a mirror, kisses a picture of the Madonna – she rushes to the garden again and maniacally mows the lawn. Stamps looks like a boy from a Carravaggio painting. The maid tries to gas herself. She goes to her room, lays on a bed, Stamp appears, she shows him her ageing cunt and he fucks her.

There is a boy (the son) in pyjamas – Stamp gets naked, muzak playing, the boy wants Stamp to fuck him, the boy hesitates, he bungles, Stamp feigning sleep, cheekbones on a pillow, a fallen angel carved in stone. Silvana on the veranda picks up a book of Rimbaud's poems, she looks at the photo of Rimbaud on the cover and thinks of her son... Stamp is touching the boy's shoulder.

'Are they going to do it?' Rez wonders excitedly. Silvana's wig is looking more like a Guinea pig with each shot. She picks up Stamp's discarded Y-fronts and sniffs them. She's wondering how big his prick is. He's slept with the entire family except her. Pasolini loves to see Stamp naked. 'YES!' Rez thinks, I want to be a movie star.

Silvana becomes mannequin-like. She is demented because she hasn't fucked Stamp. She gets into her mini sports-car. Cruising she picks up a blond boy... in a hotel room he fucks her on the bed, she turns to stone, because he isn't Stamp. She plays maternal with her lover. She disassociates from the action, which makes the boy want to fuck her more. Rez is enthralled.

Silvana, unsatisfied, jumps in to her sports car, and cruises some more, picks up two boys... they drive into the countryside and fuck her in a ditch... Stamp goes away forever.

Rez absently turns off the TV. His mind woolgathering.

Ms Thing's life in the back of the cab became like the plot of a bad thriller movie. She was seized by a flash of inspiration: she asked the driver to take her to Moscow Central Station, where she purchased two one-way tickets to Berlin. She and Rez were going into exile.

Ms Thing looked at the tickets and tomorrow's departure as a new chapter... the cab pulled up outside the apartment.

"The World is a sickening place," she sighed.

In this limbo before the journey, the hours were strewn with melancholy. Ms Thing hung in the air, carefully cogitating about her future as the patron saint of street trash and rent boys — transvestite deity of the dispossessed.

Chapter 10

The Disintegration

For Ms Thing and Rez everything now breaks down into dream, death and sex. One is watching the film of their lives spill out of the projector onto a never-ending floor. Rez is on the edge of the ledge.

This whole story reeks of sperm, dream and delusion. Images take over as words fail, or as belief in them does.

In a dark moment – a corner of space – dark green train doors slam. Rez asleep in the couchette. Before me I see Ms Thing on a yellow road made from the gelatin of Nembutal.

I see Rez becoming like Genet's Querelle immortalised in Fassbinder out-takes.

Ms Thing, sick thing. Rez was bored by her, her coprophiliac suppers, endless picnics of excrement, her sickening squelching anus: sick of her cage, her depraved conceits.

What a disintegration, breaking down of boundaries into… what? Further into aberration, until… what?

Is the text, their text, just a long strand of spit, dripping into a pit?

MEDEA FIXATION: Ms Thing wraps herself in a red shawl, preparing for their departure.

She is a creature of silent screaming, she (in her mind) runs across arid landscapes, casting her shadow in doubt. She feels like Medea, losing Rez, her Jason, to a younger queen. And the queen will be the city of Berlin.

Ms Thing muttering to herself:

"I hear sailors talking about horizon lines and comparing them to the contours of their lover's bodies. 'He's a dip in the north' 'She's curved like the cape of good hope'. The state of things, the state of things, I'm not what I once was, I'm coming apart at the seams... I have lived a life of constantly shifting selves... and now this boy, his presence, has taken me into higher, yet darker, plateaux, his cock-meat has pulverised me into death, he is my angel of the abyss, the more he came in me the nearer I come to death, his disease, his youth... I am infected." Here she stopped muttering, dribble sliding down her lips.

Inside Ms Thing's head a film played, in the form of Pasolini's *Medea*, starring Maria Callas. Ms Thing as Callas as Medea.

She hears tinkling Balalaika music, she is drowning in this vision... her lungs ache, stabbing pain in her heart, her eyes dart from side to side, she cries: "Jealousy is the cause of everything".

A little boy rides on the back of a Centaur, is it Jason or is it Rez? Ms Thing confuses the two identities.

"Nothing is natural," she whines.

She is looking back on her time with Rez like a maniac film actress viewing the day's rushes of her latest film, avidly, wildly watching each frame.

"This is the way to exorcise my bitterness," Ms Thing declares.

Only there is no director, no sensitive Pasolini to guide her through this holocaust of self-destruction. The blue sky she sees above her head is in fact the blank screen of an Apple Mac. Words, sentences, pour through her matted hair like syrup.

Ms Thing sees a beautiful boy trying to hang himself in a cave, that resembles Gruyere cheese. The ceremony begins. Pasolini has chosen the sexiest sacrifice – the boy in the cave is dragged out across a parched terrain, smiling until he recognises his fate.

Medea's (Ms Thing's) profile cuts a crimson arc through the desert. A priest appears and fastens the boy to a cross of wooden bars, the priest anoints the boy's chest, shoulders, side of his face. The beautiful boy giggles as the priest's hands slide over him, coating every muscle in milk (Pasolini's pick ups: Italian boys he used like confectionery – like toilet paper). The priest strangles the boy just into unconsciousness, then mutilates him into little pieces... Ms Thing screams, "No it's not Rez, it can't be Rez, not Rez."

The boy, not Rez, but enough like Rez to torment Ms Thing, is dismembered, torn, the congregation eat his body parts, smear a tree with his blood... he's a feast.

In a pit, Jason stands with Medea, their masks are the faces of Ms Thing and Rez. They freeze. Little figures dressed in black, carrying huge eggs, dash about. Does this represent the future unborn?

Ms Thing commands no one in particular but with grand gestures intones: "Prepare me for the temple".

She is now chained to her role and her symbol is fire.

Diamanda Galas enters the scene in the back of little red sports car, brandishing a jagged edged dagger, playing Callas playing Medea. Ms Thing suddenly feels like a supporting player in her own drama. Diamanda says, "There's only one queen allowed in this room dear, and you're not it."

Ms Thing is affronted by Galas, who vaguely reminds her of the Countess Handover.

Diamanda: "You've never really suffered. My brother Dimitri died of AIDS, his pain was unsung, unheard, and when he died it was like someone had turned out all the lights, and all I could see was red, a red sea of contaminated blood issuing out of arses, cunts, fingertips, eyes: tears of blood."

Ms Thing had had enough – she fast-forwarded Diamanda.

She was cogitating in a cold passion under a Nembutal sun.

"NOTHING IS POSSIBLE ANYMORE," she shrieked in a poor imitation of Diamanda.

Bored, the couple board the Trans-Psyberian Express to Berlin. It's night. It's snowing. A percolating sorrow washes over them. They are leaving Moscow for the first and last time. In Poland the train will stop to let a herd of Cows lick melting ice off the tracks.

Slithers of icy moonlight inside the red velvet couchette, tiny room, heart-shaped – bunk bed in black satin, black lace at the windows – a funeral chamber. Rez is hot and takes his top off, she revels in his musculature, panting very quietly. She casually slings his rucksack on the floor along with her valise. Beauty and the beast in baggage form.

The Trans-Psyberian Express shunted into the night.

Ms Thing's and Rez's subconsciousnesses struck up a dialogue. They slumped into a light doze. The train's motion sending them nodding, the deepest part of themselves were in accord and the couchette, like the apartment, became their chamber and they never left it.

Ms Thing: "Oh Rez, am I, as all queens, bound to suffer?"

Rez: "We are dying, we are floating, you are my anchor on reality."

Ms Thing: "I knew your Mother, Rez, she used to work as our maid at the Iron Cervix."

Rez: "Everything seems like a dream, like my past doesn't belong to me... I'm trapped in Nembutal Land, everywhere I turn, I run back into myself."

How truthful and powerful their subconsciouses are. How poetic, and out of time their words are. Yet Ms Thing couldn't keep her mind off sex for very long. She inserted two fingers into her rectum and began masturbating...

Ms Thing: "As we got on the train and you went to the toilet, I saw a gorgeous young man get on board, he was listening to a

Walkman. Tall and lean, high cheek bones, melting brown eyes, intense – I could trace the lines of his biceps under his jacket sleeve, and follow the line of his pectoral muscles under his tight black polo neck sweater. He was a vision. Brown hand glinting on the silver door knob. I looked down at his crotch – a grey area – holding many secrets. I wondered what he looked like when he came. I thought of you my dear Rez... I must have swooned... he wouldn't look at me, but he knew I was drinking him in... I was glowing in his beauty – a reflected glory – but I didn't want to know anything about him, because he wasn't you."

Ms Thing was flooding everywhere.

Rez says philosophically: "I think I have learned that in this world we blend into many forms – we are all each other; we are one and we are many... Many contained in the one. We are angels and we are devils, and we are lights of joy, we are shadows of despair... before long nothing will matter and that will be magnificent. Our dreams are the keys that dissolve the ice in our hearts – only *nothing matters now*. Every single thing that charms us is ourselves."

Ms Thing cut Rez off with more of her anxieties:

"I'm a lady in waiting: waiting for decrepitude. For I am decrepitude in all its splendour manifest. Bedazzling. Under the wrinkles, the crow's-feet, under the bags and cascading dewlaps, agreeable to the eye or not... I'm like a scab, which, if you picked away at, you'd find under it the dried blood-threads of pus." Still masturbating, it takes her a long to achieve anything near a climax – her prostate... a withered nut.

The candle-light flickered in the couchette. Snow furled past the windows in white Polar bear clouds. The pair's subconscious dialogue abated. The turning of the wheels, the clickity-clack sound over and over caused in a tiny panic to set in.

The panic transformed into lewd ponderings about the young man on the train. Suppose he burst into their couchette and demanded filthy sex – what a scintillating idea!

Her passion is ignited by the imagined stranger as he strips for them: brown fudge skin and a delicious cock awaits Ms Thing's fumbling. Ms Thing is deep in fermentation. She looks over her shoulder as the young man – call him THE STRANGER – is about to penetrate her anus.

"Deign, my love, to thrust your cock into my stinking hot bowels. Fuck-meat... so thick! You must pound my guts." She imagines the stranger now ramming her good and proper, Rez is turned on, hot, pulls out his cock and goes behind the stranger and spits in his hand, as the stranger rams harder, Ms Thing is being pushed down, Rez enters the stranger, two rams in a chain reaction...

Rez searches for the stranger's nipples whilst his cock is pumping away, he glides his fingertips over the stranger's chest until he finds the nipples smooth and textured like the skin of plums, he pinches till rivulets of blood stream through his fingers. The stranger's torso wet with sweat and blood, in this frenzy he is brutally impaling Ms Thing, plunging into her hole so violently that torrents of shit run down her legs. The stranger withdraws and goes down and starts sucking up the shitty flow... Rez, completely psychotic now, pins Ms Thing to the floor, on her back, and rams his cock into her mouth, knocking her two front teeth out. She looks like a dead horse. Rez is fucking her teeth... back of her throat. The stranger's face is caked in shit and blood, he pulls Rez's arse into his face and plunges his tongue deep into Rez's hole... the stranger loses his tongue... Rez explodes down Ms Thing's gullet, spraying her lungs, she turns purple with pleasure, the excess of semen spilling out of the sides of her mouth as she gasps and pants for air. The stranger flips Rez onto his back and shoves his bruised cock into Rez who instantly comes again, the stranger catches the shower in his mouth. He's fucking Rez so hard he can feel his cock on a journey inside – swelling and slithering around the boy's intestines, and finally piercing Rez's belly, shooting out of his navel – a spume of blood and come.

Ms Thing was so hot. She pulled the two fingers out of her anus and looked at the buttons of shit stuck to them... hyperventilating, her thoughts as ever mingling sex with death, popped them into her mouth. Ms Thing had entered her 'Requiem' period.

"My death, my death, my death," Ms Thing sang to herself over and over like a bleeding round Robin. "I shall not cheat my death, I shall embrace my last breath." "MY DEATH," she says out loud, the words hit the wall of their chamber and bounce just once to slither finally down to the floor, leaving a black oily stain on the Persian rug.

"My death is black and yellow – made of gelatine and narcotic powder: of tulips that turn into cocks, dripping with bitter nectar. Black ash falls upon my dead eyes."

Ms Thing had fallen in love with the idea of her own death. And actually I'm quite tempted to take a trip across to the other side, to the nether regions, to take a look with Ms Thing – at how things are on death's side.

IN DEATH – Having a look around.

Death: like a Doctor's waiting room, walls of membrane, general sense of spaciness, airy, bloodless, a bottomless pit. Ms Thing has a notion to be embalmed in Rez's jissom.

Perhaps a few fallen angels and saints loiter about, some with bloodshot eyes. Others fidget with worry beads.

One saint turns to the another and says, "No-one owns life but anyone who can pick up a frying pan owns death."

Another saint declaims, "We must triumph over misery and degradation."

Suddenly death is full of chattering saints. A leaning saint whispers in Ms Thing's ear, "We never know how much we learn from those who never return."

The taste of ashes floats up. A choir boy chokes to death on a cardinal's cock... right before our eyes... The cardinal strangles himself with his rosary beads.

A saint with a chip on his shoulder interjects through pursed lips: "I mistrust the medical profession, they lie about disease and death... all that preventative stuff is an effort to cheat death and prolong life. If you ask me it's just an excuse to get people hooked on morphine. Even the nurses are at it. Lady Diana Cooper, a most famous morphine addict, became so while working as a nurse in Flanders during the first World war."

Another saint, vibrating with rainbow colours, rambled on... "And the great Edith Piaf, after her third car crash, was given large doses of morphine to quell the pain, then became addicted. Yes, the medical profession have a lot to answer for. Why don't they tell people the truth about their illnesses, you know, 'Well, Mrs Blahblah, I'm here to tell you that it's fatal, I'm afraid.' Let the patients know the facts so they can choose about their life or death."

A saint with no nose and chapped lips barked, "Talking of morphine, have any of you tried morphine suppositories? They're a wow!"

Ms Thing couldn't believe there were so many saints: saints without a cause, saints of nothing: just talking heads with nowhere to go. Perhaps the saints were nothing more than mirages or guides to oblivion.

Ms Thing, the oblivion seeker, seeking oblivion in a playground of saints.

The Psyberian Express wends its way across the cold wastes of Psyberspace – from Poland to the borders of Germany. Dawn light. Rez zonked.

In the cabinet de toilette, Ms Thing's nose is pressed to the frosted glass window. Grey light, wax drips.

Ms Thing is enchanting death sitting on the potty, she with arms open and legs closed (for a change) is welcoming remoteness and annihilation. She has swallowed 100 Nembutal.

Pictures in her dying mind of Berlin after the war: the place looked like the face of the moon, all reduced to rubble. She sees in her mind's eye... burning flesh...

"I'm walking the streets of Berlin: Friedrichstrasse, Kurfstendam, in a dream, spinning out from time, I'm a Russian trampling through a desert of bricks."

Rez, asleep, dreaming too, of melting ice (freedom) and of finding a swan curled up hidden in a hole above a curtain rail. The bird made of cotton hisses, snaps its beak, unfolds like a paper bloom. Is the swan a symbol of Berlin?

Ms Thing is on the toilet, knickers lumped about her swollen ankles, 'pillows' entirely deflated. She looks blearily into a little compact mirror, sees her face in hideous close up, well, only the bridge of her nose and leaky mouth daubed in a final swipe of Jungle Red lippy. No eyes!

She is aghast at what she sees – bags and lines – a moment of truth. Recognition glares back at her... she is chasing saints again. Her final wish? We can only guess. Perhaps she'll ascend to a beautiful white light, an enormous halo held by muscle-bound angel boys, blowing each other's trumpets. Nembutal powder poisoning her blood system: no white light as yet. Ms Thing is leaving us in a manner she would've liked, fantasy mixed with sordidness.

Her journey: up or down? Only a terrible emptiness is felt. Her final resting place on the toilet, white swirling lavatory waters below... receiving dolly's fluids that gush out of every orifice... she is empty... just a husk... eyes roll... (Maybe I should quicken her demise, send a psychotic angel boy in there with a fire hydrant to bludgeon her to a pulp, rather than let this slip, slide away).

Rez twitches in his sleep.

"Well, she was a fool to herself," I can hear the Countess Handover drawl on hearing the news of Ms Thing's demise.

Part 4

"Berlin Boy"

Shhhhh, he's sleeping

Bored Game

The old writer and I finally meet, in a landscape of shifting locations.

In a wood panelled room the walls seem to be made of corrugated iron, like a bunker. Eerie soundtrack of a boogie woogie piano plays at a slow speed. We sit around a card table the three of us: the old writer, a young unidentifiable stranger and me. On the table a board game, Mayan chess.

The old writer sits, his eyes partially shaded by a visor, like he's the card dealer, nattily dressed in a light blue shirt and tie. Is this a film noir? A dream sequence from a film not yet shot. We three sit looking at each other and the atmosphere in the bunker becomes hyperreal. Like it compresses down with malevolent energy. The old writer breaks the silence.

"I always knew I'd end up in someone else's fiction, Goddamit! Why won't you younger writers leave me the hell alone." The old writer growls, mouth twitching, narrowing his pinned eyes, sniggering he produces a hypodermic filled with a phospherescent light blue syrup.

"One of you two wanna try this?" says the old writer with a conspiratorial sneer. Some telepathic message tells me it is the Mexican hallucinogenic drug – yage.

My subliminal thoughts sew up any idea of anyone but me trying the drug, not the stranger or the old writer who appears to be preserved in the stuff.

"I will," I say.

"Gooood, it'll clue you in." drawls the old writer.

I take the syringe and without a tourniquet deftly mainline the phospherescent syrup, it's an instant hit! Multidimensional images crash in my mind, all my senses catapult, disconnecting nerves rewiring my system, my teeth feel like they're grinding down into powder... at the same time it feels very ancient, like I'm being plugged into... Words fail me...

Suddenly, on the table the Mayan chess set comes screaming to life, miniture gods and high priests cavort across the board, leaving trails of blood and tiny ripped out hearts in their wake... Humwawa appears, his face a mass of steaming offal, reeking of decay, spewing out poison gasses, Ixtab goddess of hanging lynches one of the priests, watching him wriggle, exhuming a final breath... waits for Xolotl lord of rebirth to reincarnate him so she can hang him over and over again.

The old writer chuckles and says, "you're in."

As I return to 'normal' from the cartoon of death, I notice something in my consciousness has definitely changed. I've tripped over, I've gone to the same level, the same psychic plateaux as the old writer, an initiation of some sort. A realm wherein I now recognise the unidentifiable stranger, the third party, I gaze across the table, the corner of my vision is streaming white light, the stranger is my own creation.

It is Rez.

Chapter II

The Birth of Berlin Boy

S O REZ IS ALONE, AND MAYBE THIS IS SOME CAUSE FOR CELEBRATION. A wake perhaps?

Rez becomes Berlin Boy the moment he puts his feet down on the cement platform of the Zoo station – Berlin. A rebirth. He's like a deliciously muscled phoenix rising out of the snows and narcotic powders of Ms Thing, Moscow, the past. Rez born *now* as Berlin Boy.

The city, once ruined, is now like one huge building site, being rebuilt for the 21st century. Berlin, as well Berlin Boy, is being reconstructed.

Rez reinvents himself, begins again, but what does he wear? He wears a navy blue cap with gray woollen scarf and sailor's jacket, army boots, jeans... these are the garments Ms Thing left him with... and a bundle of German marks.

Berlin Boy wanders along the platform of Zoo station, the concrete and steel yawn before him. Dust dazzles and hangs in the air. A woman wearing a leopard skin coat with two great danes walks past, trailing another time behind her... 1923? 1931? Perhaps she is meeting a lover from the train, some Russian Count or whatever... the city of Berlin, an ever shifting hologram of time changes. Berlin Boy (not Rez) spits, his signal of arrival. He leaves the station. Berlin looks like a huge fancy cake. An old bag lady staggers past... this he can't stop.

Memory: Ms Thing slumped on the loo in the couchette, how he nearly pissed on her (which wouldn't be the first time)... she looked like a cracked egg, her mouth turned up at the corners in an effort to smile her final smile. What was that last smile about? What could have amused her in the death throes? The sight of herself in the full length mirror on the back of the door?

Berlin Boy looking for a new direction:

Across the road, he sees a neon sign "Cafe Eden Eden Eden." He fiddles about in his pockets and, pulling out a wedge of German marks, crosses the road and enters the cafe.

The walls of Eden Eden Eden are yellowing, the place is in a haze of cigarette smoke. Little tables and bentwood chairs. Along the back wall there's leather sofa seating with red and gold topped tables. The place is practically deserted except for two sets of couples. The first couple: two bald men with grey handle bar moustaches – pure Kaiser.

The men are eating boiled eggs, peeling off the shells with bored expertise. They look at Berlin Boy, their moustaches twitching.

Berlin Boy passes to a table at the back where two strange but interesting looking women are sitting. One woman is slumped against the other, she has long reddish hair with bangs veiling her eyes, her face a pale sunken globe, lips swollen, eyes beneath the bangs... cracked green marbles – she is swathed in black. Berlin Boy notices a silver chain with a skeleton's head on it around her neck. A cig burns between her fingers. She is gazing at the floor. The other woman is somewhat younger and very skinny, tangled black hair – bony face like a horse. She sits in a grey vest, bits of black ribbon tied around her wrists... she is fidgeting, but listening intently to the other woman.

Berlin Boy sits at the next table to them, they pay him no mind, lost in their conversation. Berlin Boy wonders who they are. He orders a cappucino from a midget waiter in a pinstripe suit, the little fellow can hardly reach the table.

The two women are Nico and Patti Smith.

Nico turns to Patti, their hair collides and tangles together like seaweed – the waves in their heads crash into one big narcotic ocean:

Nico: "What am I going to do, Patti?"

Patti: "Well I'll get you a new one, don't worry."

Nico: "But if I don't have my Harmonium, I can't work, then I can't get my drugs... can't live."

Nico is looking panicked.

Patti: "Listen, I'm doing a gig tonight, so tomorrow I'll have some cash and we'll go harmonium shopping."

Nico: "Oh no, really, I can't take from you."

Patti: "No problem, it's a gift, I'd like to buy you something,
          you're my heroine."

Patti sneezes, peppering the table with globs of danish pastry.

Nico: "You're so kind, like a sister, no?"

Patti: "I could even get some great Iranian smack later, my
          roadies could be out scoring now."

Patti twists her hair, corkscrew around her index finger.

Nico (with tears in her eyes): "You're like a mother to me, you
          know my mother died in an asylum... I think one day I
          shall go mad... Berlin after the war... just a brick!"

Patti: "Nico, ummm, what was Jim Morrison like in the sack?"

Nico: "I lost all my money at the roulette table, Silvana said
          she'd pay my debts..." (Nico on the nod for a few
          moments.) "Jim... oh, he was a very poetic fuck... very
          Rimbaud."

Patti (who is masturbating): "OH, WOW!"

Nico: "But Brian Jones was the dirtiest fuck ever, you know he
          liked it the Turkish way – up the arse – he put a revolver
          up my cunt."

Patti is masturbating furiously – Nico doesn't seem to notice or care.

Nico: "Iggy was OK, I taught him to lick cunt... Andy
          Warhol was always watching in the shadows."

Patti (nearly coming): "And Hendrix, did you fuck him?"

Patti comes quick and orders a bottle of champagne.

Nico: "Patti, I don't suppose you have, by any chance, a little
          bit of hash?"

Patti hands Nico an eighth of Afghan hashish under the table. Nico inserts it up her bum, grimacing. Berlin Boy sits spellbound. Patti catches his eye and smiles, which in turn makes Nico look in his direction. Her stares pass straight through him.

> Nico (in her deepest voice): "He looks like that fucking Alain
> Delon – like Ari." Tears fall down her face. Patti
> squeezes her arm reassuringly.
> Patti: "Don't Nico, don't."

Berlin Boy is sipping his coffee, violet eyes peering over the rim of the cup.

> Nico: "But the days... just go... on and... on... you know that
> fucking Leonard Cohen nearly broke my wrist."
> Patti: "I've been thinking about ART – which is R-A-T – all
> things cannot transmute into art, some art must
> disintegrate into pure shit – like Brancusi, the sculptor,
> he took the solid form and made it move, made stone
> curve like a plastic smile."

Patti lights a cigarette and blows out a gust of smoke. Berlin Boy sees a cascade of tumbling horses fall onto the cafe's floor. Nico is elsewhere.

> Nico: "But I guess I loved Jim the best you know, that's why I
> always sing his song 'The End' at the end of my

shows… you know Patti, I think Jim lives inside of me, I
think that when he died he passed into me."

Patti: "The same with Hendrix, I've been fucking with him in
the past, so I can fuck him in the future."

Nico: "I couldn't fuck a black man… I… was… raped… by a
black army sergeant… and he was hanged."

Patti: "Black guys are the best! I wanted to be black… but
rapists should have their balls cut off and fed to them."

Nico laughs for the first time. "HO. HO. HO. HO. HO."

Berlin Boy's ears suddenly prick up – overhears the two bald men:
One says: "Oh, come down off the trapeze and into the sawdust.
The other replies: "That's circus talk!"

Berlin Boy feels dreamy and well in his new skin, in this new
city – watching this scene:

Nico: "But Patti I'm only really happy when I have my smack,
you know, I have too many thoughts, and the drugs slow
me down… I'd like to be a robot."

Patti: "I've written a song for you, it's called 'Dancing Barefoot'
I'm going to sing it at my show tonight."

Nico: "Sooo fan-tas-tic, Lou wrote a song about me, so did Iggy
and now you, *wunderbar!*"

Nico gets up to go and sways a bit – they kiss four times on the
cheeks. Patti waves the bill in the air and smiles at Berlin Boy. Nico
gathers her black shoulder bag and wanders away. Patti looks a bit
sad and says, "Nico, tomorrow, the harmonium." Nico looks back

and nearly smiles, "and the parties..." she booms in that fog horn voice. Patti zeroes-in on Berlin Boy.

"You from around here?" she asks.

Berlin Boy, shy, tells the truth: "I've just come from Moscow."

Patti: "I like your accent". She's cruising him.

Berlin Boy puts his guard up – he doesn't want to become involved with any more weird women after Ms Thing and Countess Handover.

Patti lights a fag and walks away, she looks back at Berlin Boy – who resembles a Robert Mapplethorpe still. Before she goes through the doors of Eden Eden Eden she turns to Berlin Boy and shouts, "TOTAL ABANDON!" and is gone.

Berlin Boy wanders the streets of Berlin – which are shadows and pockets of lights – which resemble his mind... He walks along the Meinekestrasse and checks into a double room at the Hotel Pension Imperator. The hotel room at the top of the building is decorated in ghastly 1970s brown and orange geometrical shapes – triangles with eyes on them serve as wallpaper. Berlin Boy plops down on the bed and goes blank. Being alone is like being reborn. He picks up the remote control for the T.V. and channel hops... *flick*... Marianne Faithfull singing 'Broken English'... *flick*... to commercial for chocolate truffles entering red lips, creamy fondant dripping down the models chin... *flick*... a wrestling match: two blond burly men slinging each other about groaning and grunting... *flick*... porn... bearded man takes a brunette women from behind, squeezing her tits, now fucks her up the arse... *flick*... the Wall... *flick*... news footage of skinheads rioting, smashing shop windows, setting fire to Turkish women and children... *flick*... a Spaniel jumps through hoops... *flick*... cow's behinds, tails swish... *flick*... ironing board... *flick*... Ms Thing's dead bloated face balloons out of the T.V. screeching like a Owl. Berlin Boy jumps out of his skin, digs about in his rucksack for a calming Nembutal or two.

A swim in the Nembie haze, Berlin Boy smokes a Malboro. He keeps a journal – a sort of scrapbook. It is a little black book with a red hammer and sickle on it. He doodles and occasionally writes in it.

A page from his book, coffee stained and ash smudged, a doodle of a horse – a cappuccino horse, followed by today's entry: "We are all born mad... some remain so... I'm writing this down to assert myself, to know myself outside of who I am... have become."

What a blossom he's become. It is I that puts a neon halo above his head which shimmers "Berlin Boy the Legend". His flesh like pages of a calendar – days turn to dust.

Berlin Boy looks down at the cappuccino horse which swirls around the page dumping specs of chocolate manure... his eyelids slope, the blinds to his dreaming mind are down.

He enters a nap – a dream of ice – back then – as Rez.

Ice melts, an invasion. Borders bleed into one another, continents merge and the common state is one of suspension. The bowels of the ship slowly filling up with the murky waters of the Okhotsk ocean... the ship spinning... everything adrift... tears turn to tidal waves – then to ice. Rez / BB is split into many pieces. Each ice cube a different facet. Perhaps he dangles from the anchor under the sea, as shoals of fish nibble his earlobes.

Now the ship is on fire – Rez is leaping into the briny, overboard to obscurity, into the depths, a blank screen, a blue nothingness.

One hand dragging through the water connecting currents of future uncertainties – the belief in the future is the belief in uncertainties. What is known, and what is left to discover, can be found in a puddle of water – melted ice.

SHIP WRECKED?

In the dream, Berlin Boy stands in a pool of sea water, like Narcissus gazing at his reflection, talking to himself, watching his mouth move out of sync…

"It's like I've slipped out of one skin and into a new one. I don't know what face to wear. When awake I'm narcoleptic… But freedom… in reinventing myself? I have never learned what love is… only it seems like death." Here in the dream, oh the dream, BB's lips swell so he looks like a fish… "My symbol is a skull and cross bones wrapped in a dollar bill and sealed in semen."

The dream ends in a puff of pink smoke.

Some kind of inner voice is telling me that Berlin Boy is irretrievably lost and most certainly knows it.

Chapter 12

MOUNTAINS OF CIGARETTE STUBS AND A SNIVELLING ENNUI attempt to entice Berlin Boy to leave his hotel room and dash out onto the streets. But he delays. Out of the midnight blue a suffocating feeling crept over him, he flushed, turned grey – it was old Mama Grief that took him by the shoulders and embraced him. The delayed shock of life without Ms Thing. An uncontrollable anguish dribbled through him, as though the past had suddenly rose up to conspire against him. Barb withdrawal! What fresh hell is this? He had run out of his supply, no secret stashes to be found, none lurking in the corner of a pocket. He had been gulping them down for so long now, that even an hour without them caused the cramps... he wanted to run out and score, but instead he hit the floor – TIMBER!

There he lies on the floor, sweat gushing out of every pore, belly bloating, a thousand knives twisting and cutting at his tripe, his spleen. His beautiful violet eyes rolled up into his head, looking at his brain on fire. He rolled around crunching himself up into a little foetus-shaped ball, and then uncurled again – a dying bloom. Lying on the floor, it is raining coins – howling like an animal caught in a gin trap. About to burst. Cums repeatedly in his jeans... William Blake's 'Ghost of a Flea' prances about the room.

I can feel the shooting pains ripping through his body, he's upon the wrack... help him, help him, help help him, help him, help help help him...

Berlin Boy I want you in the headlines – a household name. I'm throwing a gauntlet down (in the form of a black leather glove with tassels) it's time for Berlin Boy to swallow his past and pucker his lips and wear a leather belt round his hips, to stop his knees shaking, cheeks flaming. I'll spit on his misfortune from a great height.

I can see him, thinner now, wasted looking – take away most of his brawn and give him a svelte figure, make him a bit fey. Berlin Boy with just a trace of black eyeliner around those weird violet peepers. Berlin Boy in a flimsy shirt and tight jeans – jeans that are painted on. Eager, mean, lean, believable. He's practically coming off the page, crawling from the wreckage of this text – his monumental cock appears through a hole in the page, followed by the rest of his lean body, until, finally, he stands behind me dictating what follows. THIS IS MADNESS... but I must continue...

I can see Berlin Boy and myself standing side by side in a mock wedding ceremony, bound in chains of words, useless words, such as 'haberdashery' or 'binder'. Dead flowers and broken promises, standing before no one in a certain perverse lunacy, holy, holy, holier than anyone – the blood red tip, ring of shit, knowing it's better to reign in hell than to serve in heaven.

I think I've finally gone… gone to pieces.

Chapter 13

"*THAT WHICH DOES NOT DROP OUT OF THIS WORLD, HERE IT remains; and here too, therefore, it changes and is resolved into its several particles; that is, into the elements which go to form the universe and one's self.*" – Marcus Aurelius.

Thus Berlin Boy came together to fall apart.

And later:

The telephone rings in Berlin Boy's room – the now svelte yet soggy boy scrambles out of his purgatory and stumbles to answer it. He picks up the shiny black receiver – looking down at an awesome hard-on.

Berlin Boy: "HELLO."

Telephone: "ABORT, RETRY, IGNORE, FAIL." The voice sounds as though it belongs to a very small person, high pitched, lisping (Truman Capote? Gary Indiana?)

Berlin Boy looks at the receiver and places it back to his ear, fiddling with his cock…

The telephone repeats: "ABORT, RETRY, IGNORE, FAIL."

Berlin Boy, more annoyed now than scared, goes to slam down the phone and continue his wank, but the voice shrieks… "No! wait! GO… to the Baa Bar… on the Kreutzbergstrasse…" CLICK… silence.

'Oh, more weird shit,' Berlin Boy thinks as he comes in his fist.

The Baa Bar was yet another dull, pedestrian gay bar, uniform in its thumping Techno music and black-and-chrome metal surfaces. Packs of gay boys, all worked out bodies and bovine brains, looking for meat and murder and sex, sex, sex. Berlin Boy was feeling better, if not stronger, he was over the worst of his barbiturate withdrawal, yet stricken with anticipation as to the meaning of the cryptic message relayed over the phone. Berlin Boy sat on a bar stool as two swishy queens sauntered past, cruising. The two queens perched on nearby stools and began conversing:

"I'm dreaming of a red Christmas and of a car crash with Boyzone," said one queen to the other.

"And how about wearing their 'bits' as a false moustache, a la Marie Antoinette, I've told you that story, girlfriend, about Marie – haven't I?" The first queen looked a bit nonplussed, the poppers having curdled her brain.

"Well dear, after she was publicly executed, some French Count, the Count de Villejuif, tore off Marie's minge and draped it over his own moustache and paraded it up and down Boulevard St Germain… a true beard!"

The two swishy queens dissolved into grey puddles of laughter.

BB surveyed the queer terrain. He felt like a meaty bone, thrown into a pack of hungry hyenas... the place was all eyes, eyes on him... the clientele shifted about, like farts etched in flesh.

Above the bar upon a shelf, in an old Pharmacist's decanter suspended in amber liquid, the skeleton of a shrunken mermaid. What once would have been long blond hair, was now thin straw that wound web-like around the tiny fishy frame... tail curved in the shape of a question mark. Another red herring in a bloody sea. Red sea turns to white, and to ice. All things dragging back to the past: trawler of old sorrows.

Berlin Boy, the lone wolf. The kid who dipped and dived into the abyss. His aloneness as Rez, is now, as Berlin Boy, a brooding contempt, a misanthropy.

The author asserts the moral rights to slash, rip, and burn the constraints that bind his character – Berlin Boy. We are seeking not only freedom, but also an atrocious immortality.

Berlin Boy lit a cigarette, puffed on it twice and threw it on the floor. It was his attempt at attitude.

The music pumped out of speakers shaped as buttocks – an eclectic mix of Techno-dub, Trip-hop... bleeping rhythms and disconnected whispers... "Into the pit" "Do you know where you were?" "What face am I pulling now?"

Berlin Boy was shocked that the lyrics exactly matched his thoughts, as though the songs were being made directly from his subconscious.

A sailor walked into the bar: plot, suspense, mystery, development of character, narrative criteria for shape and relevance, alternating scenes of dialogue and action.

The sailor, young, handsome, his muscles hard, supple, he wears a rose in his belt. Although his body is solid, he still has a shadow. Under his handsome mask one could detect an extremely complex and suffering heart.

Oh! the happiness of clasping in my arms a body as beautiful as his.

The sailor was a kind of floating reverie. The residue of sea dreams ebbed about him. Dolphins jumped over arcs of piss. He even smelt of salt or perhaps that smell is semen. Sea men smelling of semen. An infinity of stars swirled about his head. An anchor chained his feet.

Berlin Boy felt compelled to cast his net wide, hoping that the beautiful sailor would saunter over to him at the bar. Berlin Boy shut his eyes so that he wouldn't be distracted by his surroundings – he sent his thoughts across the airwaves, for the sailor to come over... blank... the sailor must have some internal pain that is blocking the transmisson.

Berlin Boy opened his eyes and tried for a smile, he aimed it at the sailor. The smile bounced off the sailor's chin. It had the desired effect, because the sailor looked at Berlin Boy and frowned. The frown was so deep that his eyes disappeared.

Berlin Boy slumped on the bar, his head in his hands. No meaning, everything in circles. Through the crook of his arms,

Berlin Boy saw the sailor standing next to him. The sailor emanated warmth. The bar receded.

"I've been away a long time," the sailor mumbled.

"Oh," replied BB.

Their first exchange: hidden meanings, oblique manoeuvres.

The sailor leaned in close to Berlin Boy's left ear and whispered: "I've sailed across the Indian ocean, the Pacific, the Okhotsk... on board I had my own cabin, and a pet monkey I got from Panama – called 'Flash', a furry, little moon-faced thing, who use to share joints with me. I had a Monkey on my back, friend." The sailor got out a pack cigarettes and offered BB one, as is the custom, they lit up. Was this a sign of love?

"I'm sure..." Berlin Boy trailed off, staring into the sailor's eyes he could clearly see his own reflection. He looked transparent.

"What I really wanted to be was a terrorist," the sailor continued, "for terrorism is about not being conscious, it's about letting things happen of their own accord, allowing things to rise up like a forest of cocks... terrorists never grow up... terrorists believe in nothing and everything... the ultimate terrorist believes everytime they kidnap or bomb somewhere, that they'll change nothing – they're soldiers of futility."

The sailor just seemed to be talking at Berlin Boy.

"I live at night... am unsure of my identity... being at sea... water contains memory... can recall all dreams... I'm constantly dissolving into different ports."

The sailor sort of swooned and fell against Berlin Boy, imparting an eskimo's kiss. A surge, the bulge in the sailor's woollen pants, nudged Berlin Boy's packet.

Their cocks met like two kittens in a sack – ready for drowning.

This mingling of genitals is the only cure for the loss of the sailor's identity. He's a sailor, but who is he? The sailor, not being on a ship – being on dry land with only his anchor around his feet to hold him down – he had nothing to fix him to this consensual reality. He simply verbalised his internal monologue. From isolation on the boat to sociability, the land on which he stands, was a vast imaginative leap for the sailor.

Berlin Boy was under his spell. He saw the sailor as a mirror: casting conundrums of contradictions. The sailor as redeemer, seen as an angel of mirrors.

The sailor speaks as a mirror:

"I came to Berlin when I was seventeen, I thought I'd found what I was looking for, although I can't remember what that was now... all I know is, I hate being shut up or bored. Some say that suicide, poverty, loneliness is a test, but now I no longer understand anything that is happening to me."

Berlin Boy somehow understood this and blurted out...

"We don't have to do anything, we can *do* anything we fucking well want."

The sailor didn't hear. Berlin Boy knew what he was feeling was desire, although he couldn't name it. He was, as ever, in a dreamy stasis.

Sonic Youth's 'Drunken Butterfly' blared out of the speakers, Kim Gordon yelling over and over, "Feel it deep down inside, you drunken butterfly."

The sailor says: "I've been bad and need to be punished, if I feel pain perhaps I'll know who I am."

"You want me to hurt you?" Berlin Boy asked the sailor.

"You can't hurt me… you can't hurt someone who feels nothing," the sailor added, "I'm beyond pain".

Berlin Boy applied some reason and asked; "Did you call me at my hotel?"

The sailor mumbled, sweeping a dark cloak over their meeting.

"I have a certain disregard for, ummm, life," the sailor explained, and put his lips against Berlin Boy's and kissed. Well, it was more of a sucking bite, the sailor biting through Berlin Boy's bottom lip… a droplet of black blood ran down his chin.

"That's a serpent's kiss!" The sailor grinned, his teeth stained with BB's blood.

Their fate sealed with a bite.

Their conversation came to an abrupt halt. The sailor became opaque, which only added to the hotness of his beauty.

Nearby, a geriatric drag queen done up vaguely like Eva Peron pisses into a pint glass and drinks the contents.

BB plunged his hands down the sailor's pants. The sailor's cock felt like a policeman's cosh, he squeezed it tightly, it weighed heavy in his palm… working up a rhythm with each squeeze of his prick, the sailor seemed to fade, gasp, hold his breath… Berlin

Boy kept pulling until the sailor exploded in his hand. Cupping the sperm, BB examined it closely, it froze, turned to ice, then crumbled to powder on the floor like lost treasure.

Now Berlin Boy wanted to leave and was about to when the sailor put his arm around his shoulder... BB stood rooted to the spot.

"I'm compelled to tell you last night's dream," the sailor said.

"As ever, I didn't know exactly where I was... what city or country, perhaps in the dream it was the City of Dreams. I wandered into a large tea room (the Russian Tea room in New York or The Fountain at Fortnum and Masons in London, or perhaps Mayhem in Brighton), I passed tables, strangers, I sensed an underlying panic.

I was aware of someone standing very close, and I now know that person was you!... we walked through the room and the word MILLENNIUM came into my mind... people looked into my eyes, I said MILLENNIUM out loud, and all hell broke loose... people scattered... I felt like I was going to implode... being pulled into total oblivion... as though my soul were about to be torn apart...

The people were so hysterical: weeping, moaning. Outside, the sky was black with smoke – intense heat – streets covered in refuse, shit, oil... the sea... turgid black... an old pier burst into flames and fell in the sea... sense of utter futility... this is how it will feel in the world's final moments."

Berlin Boy watched four-foot-long tears fall from the sailor's eyes, utterly wrecked.

*

Lost – the great distance between you and me – pages flap across deserted Boulevards – trees stricken with poisons. Tumble weeds, wooden shacks, tin baths… something's missing… troughs of piss overflow… eat me!… a drum beats, moments of panic. Perhaps he is back, old Pan.

Psycho fags burn out… I lost Martin, the sailor, way back, twenty years ago, tattoo on his shoulder of a rose in red and yellow… we were drunks, him and I… he'd smash anyone's face in if I asked him to… he'd fuck me on someone's floor without spit… he'd lie and I'd believe him… he went to prison and I went to Ga-Ga.

Berlin Boy gazed at the sailor, who is walking away backwards.

"Are you…" Berlin Boy can't finish the sentence.

He's drowning, really choking, in a whirlpool of conflicting emotions – rage – desperation.

"Are you he?" he sputters.

The sailor stands now in the middle of the dance floor, which is deserted. All the queers have vaporised into disease, delusion and death. In queer heaven they are known as The Baa Bar martyrs.

The sailor's final words to Berlin Boy are…

"I've been away a long, long time."

His green eyes blink off (goodbye Martin).

In a wink of a camera's flash, he is gone.

*

Blank screen – Ice.

Berlin Boy finds himself back at the Hotel. Laying on the bed, in lagoon of sweat, his mind is in deep space. The telephone in his hand… the voice on the other end is dim, far away, yet familiar…

"Hello Rez? can you hear me?… HELLO… let me hear you speak."

Berlin Boy stares at the ceiling, the blotchy off-white paint forms abstract, figurative shapes… a clipper ship, a flying horse, the wrinkled face of an angel.

THE END

About the author

Bertie Marshall was born in Greenwich, London 1960. At fifteen changed his name to "Berlin" and became part of a group of people known as The Bromley Contingent – the first group of Sex Pistols fans.

He is the author of seven plays and three chapbooks; *Schwul, The Palace Of Faux Pas* and *Master Bitch*. His many jobs have included; rent boy, drag queen, shoplifter and psychic.

Having completed a second novel *Author, Fag, Gutter*, he is currently working on a third.

MY FAULT

BILLY CHILDISH

Many books have spoken of the "human shadow" but precious few have the courage to speak straight from its heart. With painful honesty, Billy Childish does just that and in the process grows flowers from the shit. Seething with wonder and disgust, this volcanic novel sheds light on the "lie of my family".

Born into the emerging middle classes of the 1950s, Billy Childish takes us on a nightmarish voyage through a blighted childhood which culminates in his being sexually abused by a friend of the family. Stumbling onward into adolescence he exposes his desperate attempts to make sense of a world distorted by alcohol, bullies and yes men.

A legendary figure in underground writing, painting and music, Billy Childish was born in Chatham, England in 1959. After completing secondary education at 16 he entered the naval dockyard at Chatham as an apprentice stonemason. Unable to settle in work there followed an unsatisfactory spell at art school and thirteen years of unemployment.

Billy Childish has published more than thirty collections of his poetry and featured on over seventy independent LPs. He has exhibited his paintings throughout Europe. *My Fault* is his first novel.

360pp • A5 • ISBN 1 899598 06 5 • £7.95

CRANKED UP REALLY HIGH

STEWART HOME

In this controversial book, Stewart Home uses notions of genre lifted from film theory to prove that the Sex Pistols weren't a punk rock band. He follows this up by outlining a punk rock dialectic that on a compressed time-scale mirrors the growth and decay of the major political ideologies of the past century. Home offers a devastating critique of those writers who have claimed that there is a link between punk and avant- garde art movements such as Situationism. Home believes it is the triviality of punk rock which makes it a viable opponent of serious culture.

Rather than reiterating the histories of welt known groups, Home turns his attention to less well documented aspects of punk rock. As well as discussing sixties garage rock and the British, American and Finnish punk scenes of the late seventies, Home devotes whole chapters to deconstructing Riot Grrl, Oi! and the sorry saga of Nazi bonehead band Skrewdriver. Other acts covered include: Rocks, Queers, Psycho Surgeons, Nervous Eaters, Violators, Hollywood Squares, Lewd, Unnatural Axe, Mad, Leftovers, Nasal Boys, Child Molesters, Snivelling Shits, etc.

Stewart Home is best known as the author of the cult novels *Slow Death, Pure Mania, Defiant Pose* and *Red London*.

124pp • A5 • ISBN 1 899598 01 4 • £5.95

THE VOIDOID

RICHARD HELL

"The Voidoid was written in 1973 in a little-furnished room on East 10th Street. I was staying with Jennifer ("my thoughts and me are like ships that pass in the night") in her apartment down the block overlooking the graveyard at St. Mark's Church. Every day I'd take a cheap bottle of wine with me across the street to the $16-a-week room I'd rented for writing. The method was I'd keep going till I got to the end of a single-spaced page, which was pretty far. I'd wake up an hour later and have to drink a lot of water. Sometimes afterwards if I had some extra money I'd go to the pharmacy on Second Avenue and buy a bottle of codeine cough syrup and come back and lie on the cot again...

I still like this book a lot. It's smirched up with *Maldoror*, but I relished that and flaunted it because Lautreamont was my brother. In fact when I typed up the final draft, I imitated the format of the New Directions edition of his book and jammed the text in thick dark blocks inside big wide margins. I wanted to lay it all bare and expose it there; the paper sheets like settings for something, weird jewels, filthy aerial night photos, which when you looked inside them came alive. That's what I wanted. I hope it does something for you. I still can't help wishing it could do something intense."

80pp • A5 • ISBN 1 899598 02 2 • £5.95

FLICKERS OF THE DREAMACHINE

EDITED BY PAUL CECIL

As ever more people immerse themselves in cyberspace, and Virtual Reality freaks claim to have discovered the inner being, it is timely to recall the pioneering art and science of the Dreamachine. Devised in the early '60s by artist Brion Gysin and mathematician Ian Sommerville, the Dreamachine is still the simplest and most effective of all brain-wave stimulators. It is the first object specifically designed to be seen through closed eyes.

Notable Dreamachine users include William Burroughs, Derek Jarman and (allegedly) Kurt Cobain. Based on the principle that flickering light triggers brain-wave responses, the Dreamachine's impact is startling: images emerge from the dark and dreams become tangible. *Flickers* is the story of this amazing invention, a voyage into the art and magic of inner space.

This book includes full construction plans, seminal essays by Gysin and Sommerville, as well as extensive extracts from W. Grey Walter's The Living Brain, which provided the neurological theory for the first machines. Alongside these technical writings are essays by some of the artists who have worked with the Dreamachine, including Genesis P-Orridge, Terry Wilson, Ira Cohen and many others. *Flickers of the Dreamachine* is edited by Paul Cecil, the co-founder of Temple Press and an acknowledged expert on esoteric philosophy.

128pp • 210 x 210mm • ISBN I 899598 03 0 • £7.95